DEATH IS A JOKE

10 STORIES...10 PARADOXES...0 SOLUTION

ANAKIN BLOOM

To the chaos that none appreciates.

Contents

CHAPTER ONE

DEATH IS A JOKE

Vijaynagar, a semi-luxurious area in Southwest Bangalore, well known for fancy buildings, stores, and street food, harbored many minor institutions that taught computer programming to UPSC training. But, all in all, the area with well-built roads regularly occupied by young men and women in torn jeans and stiff bags, a new board- hung to a lush green tree, beside the McDonald cantine, caught the attention of all those who scurried along to eat and burp in the vicinity of their table. Just like a mutated flower in the bouquet that encourages our eyes to enlarge and make us wonder about the aliens, the words on the board were no less in competition in racing the viewer's heartbeat to a whole new level.

Feeling Alienated? Void of Meaning in your Life? Getting Suicidal Thoughts?

Don't worry! We are here to ease your way towards Death without fear.

Classes start on Monday, 21st June 2022.

Limited seats available.

Prof. Hari Sharma, Ph.D. in Philosophy. Bangalore.

Some curious eyes took it to be a joke, a prank played by jobless YouTubers. Some found it absurd and didn't forget to take its photo to distribute it online to make themselves appear quirky after being lucky to land in front of it. While exceptions in various fields of science are often shuddered as negligible, this vague and unique board's value was pursued by those exceptional people whose second option was limited to dying after imbibing glutton in the cantine.

The date need not be special to kick-start such a bizarre institution, and on the other hand, its selling point is so cruelly constructed that selecting a perfect date from an astrologer or performing a puja would only mean that rituals we perform are just an elaborate scheme to spurt out our aim, inconsiderate of good and bad.

As per the date displayed on board, early in the Monday morning, when wind still felt natural and sports shoes rumbled over the roads, Prof Hari Sharma, in his late thirties, carrying a heap of books supported by his armpit, wearing neatly pressed formal clothes carefully articulated to his trimmed beard and neatly cropped hair walks in front to open his new classroom. Nothing was out of place in the room- the size of a railway compartment, but the desks he ordered were rather small and the whiteboard on the wall was tilted without a nail on its right end. Without leaning towards impertinence, he walked against the wall and hung his degree certificate- a golden frame cut out of wood. A twitch on his lips appeared as he seemed to have found solace in the act of doing it. He took a few steps back and drew a huge breath that lasted a few seconds. Without due consideration of his expectations over the influx of his unknown hopeless, fearful, and anxious want-to-die students, he walks to the board and scribbles the number "1" on the board. As he looked back at the class, he realized that the room's spaciousness depended on the number of students, and its effectiveness would be decided on the reduction of those numbers, never to appear again...ever.

Sitting alone on a chair, scanning difficult Latin words with his radiant dark-brown eyes, his calm demeanor showing perplexity within the moment of eyes said that he was not the kind of person the student might expect to teach the art of peaceful death. His youth wasn't still un-flourished, his body was neatly maintained like a wax doll, and his straight gait combined with a rectangular face imitated the models on the advertisement banner.

He seemed not to think but read as the words moved. He relaxed, giving no regard to having a warm breakfast inside his bag. The water bottle was getting all the action in the room as he sipped it like a hungry baby.

After the passing of an unknown time, the sunlight retreated as if afraid of the man with a secret book learning the art of darkness. The act of the sun moving from one part of the sky to another seemed not to imbibe inside his head as the day got over without a student on the door. He walked back to his room and didn't forget to check if the board hung on the tree was signing for his classroom or not. It seemed perfect against the twilight interspersed with LEDs of restaurants.

The day two was the same as the first. Except for the change in the number on the blackboard, the air sensed the same nose, and light passed through the same retina.

On the third day, however, there was a knock on the door. With no change in his position, his eyes remained determined showing no haste, but he pointed his index finger to the stranger motioning him/her to wait until he finished that important line he was reading. The person with the knock was not giving up.

"Should I die here or come in?" an anxious feminine voice called from the outside.

Prof. Hari, disturbed, clenching his teeth within, finally turned at the lady frowning as he examined her.

Her shadow falling short in front of his table was straight and the trinkets of hair swiveled from left to right. As she stepped forward after Prof.Hair nodded, without expression, her face lightened to the room temperature was gleaming an extra mile from all the energy through the sunlight. Tight blue jeans and a round-neck t-shirt with a salient watch were tied to her left wrist. Black eyes and hair- ponytail, a pointy nose, and a neatly carved face with hints of lipstick made her look like a professional in the IT industry.

"So you want to die?" he asked, carefully closing his book as if dressing a newborn.

"I do," said the woman, and without asking his permission, she hastened to take a seat on the bench. " I saw your poster on the internet So...how can I get my admission? How long will it take? Have you trained others before? By the way, I thought, this was a joke, I still believe it is. Excuse me for these relentless questions, but I am just being curious."

"I can fairly guess that you are not here to die...Am I right?" he said, leaning back comfortably on his chair before the board.

"I wish you were wrong. How did you know that? Did you read my face?" her body moved forward to listen carefully as if her life depended on his words.

Prof. Hari chuckled and biting his lips said, "A person who is willing to die never asks many questions" suddenly, his face grew uncertain, it got mixed with thoughts from the mind,". So, what are you? A reporter? Or a psychiatrist?

"

"Neither!" shrugged the women.

"Then why are you here?"

"Curiosity!... I suppose"

"I am not a man to be concerned with your curiosity. If you please make your way out, it'd be really helpful"

"Are you afraid of me Mr. Hari?" she asked sitting straighter than ever.

"Should I?" answered Prof.Hari with a challenging glance.

"Not at all! I am here to know, how to die without anxiety?"

"Are you ready to die now?"

"Not now...maybe in the future,"

"You are always welcome when that future arrives. Rationally speaking it would never arrive, just like now, you will be seeking reasons as your primary instructor while deciding whether to die or not in the future. A reasonable man, no matter how messed up or drowned in the uncomprehending array of problems he may be, always comes up with a reason to hope for a better tomorrow. And now, as we have already established ourselves that you are not that kind of a person, there's no need for your unexpected welcome in the future. The future you ascribed is simply false. Maybe, exists in another reality."

The lady listened with an open mouth, called in for her mind to remind what she heard, and make her move after significant thought, "That's a smart deduction. I think I underrated you."

Smiling affably, Prof Hari said, "That's not new."

Looking attentively, the lady tried to enhance the eye contact among them, "Now tell me, Mr. Sherlock...Why are you doing this insane job?"

Prof. Hari was the master of this game, without being hesitant, he answered, "I am merely helping people do what they want. I am trying to reduce the net stupidity in this world"

"Stupidity?"

"Yes, you heard me right."

"How?"

"When a person dies, he doesn't know if he's dead or not..." he takes a sniff of the air and expels the air with a short-lived chuckle, "But when someone is stupid, even though he knows, he really can't help it but his helplessness will leave a trace of contagious stupidity. That's where I come in."

"Don't you think it's wrong? Unethical? Encouraging people to die without calling in their regrets, which could change their mind somehow."

"Death is like a joke! A joke has no meaning unless it appears on our face, unexpected, eccentric, and unbound to our natural existence. We need not be conscious while we experience a joke, it happens as it must, and so must be death."

"It's not a matter of choice?"

"I don't know,"

"You don't know?"

"Every time I hear the word, choice, it brings me closer to unnerving conclusions. It's empowering, as well as a degrading factor. You can't really rely on choice. People make bad choices all the time and my argument is quite simple...Why not let the stupid people make one bad choice of all time."

Pale and perturbed, the lady asked in a sharp resolute tone, "Do you ever think that you would make that choice?"

"I am working on it," he said calmly his face more expressive and suddenly alive.

She was dissatisfied, and looked left and right as if releasing her tension, "Who gave you the right to tell someone to die?"

"My students,"

"Where are they?" she asked, pointing to the empty seats around.

"They will come...stupid people always find a messy path" he remained calm.

"What makes you so sure? Instinct? Disbelief in the human spirit? Or simple laziness?"

"I don't know,"

"Now, let's say, for the sake of argument, I am your student."

The Professor on the other end, cognizant and excited with enlarged eyes nodded affirmatively.

"Teach me to die without anxiety."

"First of all. I want to know the way you choose to die."

"Why?"

"I want to know," he tapped his hand over the table.

"Falling off of a building maybe," she said with a softened voice.

"If it fails?" asked the Professor.

"Poison"

"If it fails?"

"How can it fail?" the lady cut in sharply, stupified with bewilderment.

Prof. Hari, with an assuring voice, said, "I want to know all your choices...that's all."

"Hanging from the ceiling...Gun...Railway track...Stabbing...River...Snakebite...Starving...I can't name more than these, I would be a psychopath if I know more."

"That's simply awesome," Prof Hari smiled, and getting up from his chair, he began preparing to leave the room.

"What is going on?" asked the lady with a cold tone.

"I am going" his voice shook as he hustled to pack his books.

"Where?" the lady kept her cold stare.

Standing up straight, the Professor walked towards the door, finally turning around at the lady, he answered, "Thank you for all those ideas. I am going to die in one of those ways."

CHAPTER TWO

DREAM NATION.

I wanted to dream and I wished to be the greatest dreamer in the whole world. If the world is made beautiful by the dreamers, why can't I strive to dream for an extra hour while others take lunch or go shopping? I got to dream big. Not for the world, but for myself.

To begin with, I am not new to this arena. My dreaming has been on the road for ten years on the same chair, and can't say that I have diverged or surprised myself with unknown horizons in this field, but I was sure of certain frames comprising of an unknown big house with a swimming pool and a luxury car, that were so repetitive that I could draw them on the sand with utmost precision. My fellow dreamers shared this very dream, and some were so obsessed that they carved the car's structure on a stone to keep it on their dreaming table. I thought I was the only one with that dream and ever since then, I crave to dream something new, something original, and something out of the ordinary.

My father, when young, prayed to god to get a dream like mine. Unfortunately, his time is done. All he can do is smile at me dreaming and pat on my shoulder to drop an extra drop of blood in the process. My mother spends her vast amount of time consoling me to dream the same dream by feeding me some special food to rejuvenate the dreaming part of my brain. She too, is in a dreaming state of her own, seeing me dream something I don't want anymore. Dreams do cost differently. There is no escaping my dream without altering the year-long transfixed dreaming state of my parents. My dream is their dream in a certain way. When I think about the escape, it appears like I am too far away from change. I feel old to grow some wings and fly on my way to nowhere. To manipulate my purpose, the past can't be shaken.

Without dreams, we have no life. With the current dream, I feel like I am one without my oneness. I have a name, but that doesn't add up to anything that is innately mine. I don't think anyone including me wants the same colors, smell, and choices in their dream world. How can we go otherwise? We were all taught to dream the same with similar uniforms from childhood.

CHAPTER THREE

TOILET THEORY OF UNIVERSE

It's been an unusual day for Dr.Ashween. All those years of contempt and heinous underestimation by his colleagues seemed to hit a dead end. Just like sweet river water that surrenders itself to the mother ocean after completing its horrendous journey-the day has come, his day of payback. He raises his timid head to feel the sky through the white ceiling. Closing his shiny eyes he concludes that the great God dilemma is going to end forever.

He whispered softly "Eureka...Eureka..." releasing his warm, happy breadth rhythmically while the dopamine and adrenaline turned busy converting his regular dull shady face into a sparkling satisfied stoic.

Wearing his rare dimpled smile, stretched close to his jawline Dr.Ashween Gnani threw himself out of his office inducing a stressed pinch to everyone around. He was a totally different man to the viewers. Even the face sensors at the corners might have been confused looking at this strange pattern on his face. He looked like he had won a billion-dollar lottery, walked like a celebrity on the red carpet and everyone's attention never seemed to overwhelm his excitement. His joy flourished through his fancy walk, the way looked clear and his enemy was expected any time soon.

"It really is my lucky day to see you like this," said Mudassir Haq with his teasing smile and continued "Did you have a date with an alien? Or did you look at any bikini woman on the beaches with that stupid telescope?".

Dr.Ashween laughed and patted Haq's shoulder looking behind his back.

"Small boy's talk..ha," Ashween answered with some seriousness "I don't have time for this shit. See you later".

Haq was embarrassed and impressed too by this competing behavior. He left the way to spread this insane act to everyone around. He was a spy assigned by bored-out colleagues to provide them with real-time information about Dr.Ashween's mood swings.

Carrying a rolled paper in his hand and a thousand thoughts popping in his mind Dr.Ashween with his shiny blue eyes is racing towards the head office to meet the President of NASA. His nose shines along the way and his dark black short hair erect with a swipe of his palm mixed with the forehead sweat were about to witness something new. His eyes were focused on the wall at the extreme end and his R&D office vanished from behind and he seemed to smell the President sitting in his chair with his favorite carrot juice "I smell victory" he said to himself and accelerates looking at the portraits of astronomic giants from Galileo to Stephen Hawking stuck to the wall.

With a few blocks left to reach the office in that huge building, the rolled paper in his hand began absorbing the downpour of sweat from his palm and the intensity of bumping thoughts increased. Among all that chaos in his head, a dominant thought rose to uphold a flag of victory and said "Lemme show these freaks what I am made of". He felt his throat turning tight preparing for a perfect conversation. Tilting his tie left and right he marched in front of the office to be stopped by a security guard in his fifties whose mustache protruded like the teeth of walrus.

Taking a step in front, the guard said casually "it would be appropriate if you could turn up after two hours". Dr.Ashween looked puzzled and the guard continued "The president is busy in a meeting with the board of directors. I am ordered not to allow even if the President's own mother arrives."

The guard has made his point and Dr.Ashween was left with no option but to withdraw his steps which went totally against his instinct. He knew that the meeting would take a whole day and in the next few days, the President would be out of the country. He had to move in but he was in no shape to face the guard physically. He stood there in front of the guard looking at the huge door making himself vulnerable to the doubts in the guard's mind. The guard with the name tag "Sheldon Raj" released his folded arms and placed one of them on the stick attached to his belt.

Instead of anger, sympathy seemed to conquer Sheldon Raj's emotions as he saw sparkling pebbles of tears rolling down from Dr.Ashween's eyes. "Are you all right sir?" asked the guard taking his hands off the stick with no response from the other side.

Dr.Ashween pressed his chest, tightly bent his spine facing the floor began faking a heart attack. It was natural and believable for his weak body and thin hands. Alerted, the guard ran towards him and sat below him looking at his reddened face. He took out his walkie-talkie and dialed for medical help. Anticipating this very moment Dr.Ashween tossed himself up, pushed the guard to the floor and ran towards the door uncontrollably, and banged on it creating a serious sound of impact only to fall back on the same side, half-conscious, too late to realize that the door was locked from the inside.

The guard who fell back stretching both of his arms like Jesus christ woke up like he was given a shock to his fading heart and ran towards Ashween.

"Are you insane? Or Do you want me to lose this job?" he cried with agitation and remembered that the medic he called hadn't gone in vain. Partially conscious of his surroundings, Dr. Ashween couldn't map out the development around him. His forehead was bulged, which looked like a soaked heap of red mud. The blunt realization that he couldn't make through that door appeared to have no compromise with the pain leading him to surrender into the world of unconsciousness.

The color white radiated around him like he was surrounded by a white ocean reflecting the white sky. He suddenly closed his eyes to have a moment for his retina to reconfigure the situation he was in. His mind was pitch black, with no thoughts except the growing anxiety.

"You can open your eyes now," a voice so pleasant and so divine came out like a God talking from the sky.

"Who are you?" asked Dr.Ashween with a stressed tone still his eyes closed.

"Don't be sad, you haven't reached heaven yet" came the same voice with a pinch of humor.

"Don't be so kind, heaven and hell are for those who are incompetent to prosper in their life" Dr. Ashween tried to open his eyes, but they shut back at the intensity of light. "Ah! This hurts"

"Being kind is my job" said the voice and came forward to massage his eyes making way for his optical neurons to make some connection with the brain.

He saw neatly arranged white hospital beds, a white curtain over the sunlit window, and a white old doctor with his white chest hair and a white coat. He began to feel his body, laying pressed to the smoothest bed. He saw his arm was attached to the saline tube, his headache was reduced to bits and the memories of facing the guard and banging the door went on like a train on his memory rails.

"How long have I been here?" he asked, and the doctor took the seat beside his bed with a mood-healing smile.

"Not how long!" the doctor said, " How many times, would make the perfect question?"

He gazed at his watch for a moment and announced that he had been resting unconscious for nearly two hours.

"Really! Two hours?" he exclaimed "I need to get back to the office, the meeting might have been over by now". He squandered the bedsheet away from his body and made a dire attempt to remove the saline only to get interrupted by the guard who stood standing there like a sculpture wearing the look of a beast watching its prey.

"If you both of done with your childish talks, can I speak now?" the guard said "The President wants to talk to you" he declared and moved back carrying the same scary stare.

Resisted by the doctor, Dr.Ashween forced himself to visit the office with saline still attached to his arm sitting in a wheelchair. Regaining his excitement that looked to overthrow all his pain along with the passing wind, he moved faster. The same path and the same portraits made him smile.

He entered the office mixed with happiness and nervousness. He rolled inside to see the President Dr. Stone, a thick black-bearded, thin-eyes wearing golden framed round glasses and a fatless stomach stuck back to the chair, in front of whom sat six board members, three on each side.

The president nodded his head twice folding hands under his armpits trying to make Dr.Ashween comfortable. He took out his eyeglasses, examined them, and wore them back. Dr.Ashween on the other hand was staring at the clock behind the President's head that was about to strike 11.

"Hello There!" the President waved his hand. "Everything all right young man?" he asked "Look, we don't mean to disturb you, if you want some rest, you can go back"

Dr.Ashween shot at once "No!", the scream echoed twice before vanishing into thin air. "I am perfectly balanced, Thank you," he said with a gratified voice and threw an awkward smile trying to ease the situation.

"In that case, define balanced?" asked the President taking a squashed paper out of his coat pocket and slapped it on the table changing his expression from active listener to skeptic filtering every word of his opponent.

It was the paper that he carried from his office, he couldn't recall the exact moment he slipped it off. As per his vision comply at present, he could see that the words on it were scattered into shapeless form due to his sweat, but the headline was still intact.

"THE TOILET THEORY OF UNIVERSE!" The President read, cleaning his spectacles rubbing them hard on his coat, then on his thighs, and finally with a clean cloth. "I suggest you spend some time with a psychiatrist Doctor Ashween, I can understand what you are going through. You stay alone, you are humiliated by your colleagues, and you spend a lot of time on that terrace. I only wish for you to not commit suicide."

There was a brief pause with everyone looking at Dr.Ashween, the clocks ticking punctuated the silence, it was singing a song, a song of destiny, and a new beginning for Ashween.

Dr.Ashween raised his head and looked confident "First of all sir, I am very comfortable being alone and if you are judging me by that paper in front of you, brace yourself, for I have everything you would be glad for you to hear."

"Are you serious?" the President picket the paper again and this time he read too loud in a sarcastic tone"The Toiled Theory Of Universe, have you got chased and bitten by a mad dog again or something?" and all the men around the table laughed on their own strength without disturbing others.

Dr.Ashween was in no mood to give up, rebuked "Our basic understanding of our universe is a lie, the chaos embedded in every particle made us draw different conclusions while completely ignoring the bigger picture."

Everyone's face was now pulled towards Dr.Ashween, they saw him with dumb admiration, confused whether to pursue his words or not, some of the bent spines were straightened.

"With due respect sir!" began Dr.Ashween "I just need five uninterrupted minutes and if I don't convince you with that theory, I resign."

These unanticipated words sent a slight shock wave around the room, like an announcement of a tornado far away from home. Everyone looked at each other with a mixed expression, but one common feature was to give him a chance, by the way, it was too interesting to let go.

The President said after nodding to the directors.

"You better make it count"

Dr.Ashween was on his own, he faced down to his feet and took a deep breath, and lifted his head up sighing as if the air was pushing it up.

‘I have a good feeling about this’ he said to himself and began addressing.

"In 1977, NASA sent a voyager installed with a Golden Record to greet the aliens right?" He looked around and realized that he shouldn’t be asking the question. Nodding himself, he continued "After 30 years, we lost its contact and we know that it is still on the move, but" he stressed "a few days ago, I witnessed strange radiation of light from the northern edge of the Milky Way Galaxy, and that is the place the voyager moved and lost its contact

"At first, I believed that it was a supernova going through an explosion, but the story was different, it looks like we have alien friends from the outer rim of our galaxy" he paused and the chatter among the directors with the President wearing unbelievable expression bent forward said, "How is that radiation of light source is even related to the existence of aliens?"

"Well! That’s where I worked on for hours," Dr.Ashween began boldly "The radiation looked simple, but it had a pattern, a pattern too difficult to realize. The colors it emitted were according to the wavelength intended to send a scripted message. It held the secret of our universe. Of course! Numbers alone can’t say a story, when I converted those digits to binary and fed them into the software I developed to decode them, the secret opened up like Pandora’s box. Looks like our alien friends are far more advanced than us."

The President asked "What was the message? Did they plan to attack earth?" he giggled closing his mouth, enjoying every moment of it.

"If they had intended to attack, considering their eminent technology, we would have been floating in the dust by now. Instead!" he shot up "Instead of attacking, they seem to worship the knowledge by sharing what they know."

Dr.Ashween had all the control, even the President was stuck as a puppet under his mind throbbing words. He found that the saline was emptying, he removed the needle and gulped half the water from the bottle. He was filled up with all the enthusiasm arising from the core of his body.

"When Galileo's vision palpitated the basic understanding of our solar system, those incredible facts cost his life. Newton's law of gravity, one of the human's greatest leaps toward astronomy was found fragile when Einstein came up with his General theory of relativity. Stephen Hawking proved that Einstein's theory broke at the point of singularity during the Big bang and a black hole. Until now, nobody knows what happened or what existed before the Big Bang. The scientific minds will be getting whiplashes by God's people until we come out with an answer. The answer so credible, concrete and can even be stupid to change the world of astronomy forever."

The speech had his air suppressed below his throat. He stood unbuttoning his collar, the wind from the fan showered the skin on his backhead, the sweat on his forehead crystallized slowly, and the warm air from his nose married with the cool wind. Dr.Ashween once again felt his voice getting brisk, and the pain of the forehead emerged when he wiped out the last of the sweat beads. His gallant figure bought an immense change in the expression of the viewers. The standing position brought with it some seriousness, and his eyes made a connection to every single pair in the room.

"The truth" he began "shall set us free. But only if we see it with an open mind"

"Come to the point" roared the President.

"The Universe we live in and study about lies in the cammod of a huge superintelligent alien species."

A fist struck the table, it was the President "What?" he screamed "Do we look like a fool to you? Are you on cheap dog drugs lately?"

"Let me finish sir! If I fail you, I am too happy to leave this organization without leaving a bad remark."

The room went silent again.

"Imagine your cammod as a universe, and the liquid at the center of it as the vast collection of dark matter, galaxies, and debris after the big bang, which inevitable says that the big bang which emerged out of infinite density is the poop coming out of butt hole".

The disgusting faces were the common reaction, some belched but none of them seemed to deny the words.

"The dark matter that wears most of the space is the liquid with extremely high molecular space making itself appear void to our naked eyes. As our galaxies and planets are so small to fit in that cammod, our time is relatively too very slow compared to that alien, which according to my meticulous calculation accounts for our 100million years as a single day in the life of an alien

"We say that the universe is expanding and the black holes suck out planets, but none of us knew where they go, it's because they are flushed inside, and 65 million years ago during the age of dinosaurs, Earth experienced an intense meteor shower taking away most of the lives. It was not a meteor"

"Oh! Shit!" The President sighed.

"Yes sir, the meteors were real shit"

The wind that was soothing all this time, suddenly turned hot, the toes wanted their skin to reach out to the world, the throats sought waters but most of all, the challenge they were put into was too absurd, as to convince a common man into believing that we live in the toilet. It appeared crueler to say that we are products of a shit.

The President asked uneasily "Are you sure about this doctor?"

"I reread the information a thousand times, and the observation fits at every inch of the reality" The faces wanted something more than his word, "What do you think about the gases we breathe and especially why were the planets hot after the big bang. It is too disgusting to imagine, but the truth often throws our expectations away from the horizon. The next meteor shower will occur after 35 million years. Next time, we need not run but close our noses." He ended with a faint smile, that was approved by every face.

"Look Dr!, Whatever you've presented here, looks too hypothetical and I'll allot a committee to go through the facts" The President assured out of the blue, he suddenly seemed concerned and satisfied "But, for now, let us keep it out of a common man's reach. Best of Luck"

The Doctor, who entered the hall from behind took Dr.Ashween back to the white bed and sedated him.

Dr.Ashween, satisfyingly murmured about his victory while drifting into a deep sleep.

The next day, Dr.Ashween was alone scribbling on a piece of paper with his new invention. After engaging himself with a wry smile for about an hour he threw himself out of his office and began walking briskly towards the President's office. Mudassir Haq interrupted as usual. Instead of conversing, he snatched the paper out of Dr.Ashween's hand, which was already wet with sweat.

"What is this, good friend?" enquired Haq, with his free hand on Dr.Ashween's shoulder.

"It's my new theory of the universe."

Haq, lowered his head curiously and went through each word,

"The Hamburger Theory!?"

Dr.Ashween took his paper and announced in a friendly tone"Come, let me explain..." he said and both of them walked away.

CHAPTER FOUR

The Secret Bath

Unable to breathe, unable to rest, and unable to give up, Kim, taking his brown, donut-shaped Ozorol soap, walked counting his steps towards the most hated space of his house. The Bathroom! Ah, Shit! Here I go again, he said to himself as if he was under a tricky curse. The dry wind swirled around his rented house and the dust trapper at the ventilation chamber was failing day by day making him allergic to the skin-tearing wind. His steps were heavy with un-understandable responsibility making him stumble into chaos at each of his decision. He looked dual the age, talked like old men with wisdom, and did this all by himself, to himself.

The floor was slippery, the walls were stained with some unknown oil, the taps were corroded with crystallized salts and the mirror was split from the center into a thousand different directions, branching until they found the silver boundary afraid of yet another strike from Kim's petrous fist. The sound of the falling water echoing all around merged with the neon light at the top of his head, which witnessed a man with his stout shoulders getting afraid while rubbing his body. Kim's hands were swift, they passed throughout his body like a cockroach getting chased by a rat. After all, it was just the beginning of his nightmare.

He thought and thought and thought, each thought, surpassing the previous with its vehemence. The brown soap in his hand was fighting for its dear life as his fingers were squeezing halfway through its body. It was then, did he realize that he has to take care of it, get used to its feathery dry scent, and preserve it and its predecessors until the end of his life. Ozorol had a shampoo too that smelled just like the soap, but Kim took care not to grow any hair. He looked odd, but he was concerned the least, except to wear a scented wig while meeting the Manager every once in six months, who visited his workplace to check his report and make up his mind to give some allowance or not.

There was only one way that he could replace Ozorol Soap. It required making a choice and signing a contract by hopping into a different workplace. There were many options, but none were particularly consolating for Kim.

The soap foamed, the water trickled and the rough body deserted with his sweat bore a sweet smell of unknown origin which any layman could inhale and say confidently that 'This hopeless man here, belongs to Ozorol'. Ozorol was where Kim worked for the past five years.

The body went red with moderately burning water and the skin on his fingers was shrinking while Kim lost sense of the surroundings drowning deep into the images of a secret bedtime story by his great grandfather passed on to each generation with rusting imaginations. Kim's mind, although stressful and delirious was going against the flow of evolution, which was erasing the ability to imagine an unknown reality that once was a part of human history.

He imagined swimming in a cool natural lake surrounded by trees where they shed flowers making it heavenly beautiful. The clouds reflected and the white birds with long beaks were hustling to catch their favorite fish. Some got hold of tadpoles and others got chased by Kim himself. The valley where the water followed bore the sun who was about to bid goodbye to Kim's part of the world. Kim's body was lean and weightless as the fishes tickled his bosom and the weeds massaged his foot. He was confident enough to swim till the horizon where the sun would appear massive blinking his final spark of light.

There were many things that Kim was fond of from his childhood. The football game with his seniors, the painting of a tea kettle with his mother, jumping on his bed trying to catch a mosquito et cetera, but none of them were as effectively attached as this imagined reality of the natural bath because of what happened next when he dreamed of it in the bathroom.

His skin began to itch, burns appeared like bubbles, and acne-like lesions made him jump to and forth until he turned off the shower. "Fine! Fine!" he shouted to the water pipe as if it were coming to eat his body- which it did metaphorically, "I won't use any more water!". He took his towel and smoothly rubbed his body trembling as it went over the boils and acne.

Kim was born white in the city of Mumbai, India, sharing his genes from an American mother and Indian father. But his body appeared sunburnt as if he was locked in an iron barrel with fire at the bottom. His eyes hated to see himself, and his nose had lost the smell of his own like the rest of his colleagues. His face was in oneness with his head, his long nose and thin lips were blended like acid-washed skin. His facial hairs were on the brink of extinction, all thanks to the tar and asphalts in the overconsumed water.

When he dressed up in the pink shirt, and black trousers with a black tie, he looked exactly like a manikin at a fashion store. He liked his dress only for the reason that it covered most of his body leaving space for some part of his face which he covered with a cap and a worn-out mask.

After having a saltless breakfast, he took the same bus at 8 every day. Along with him joined the workers from Zista, Canori, Sinqil, Hydro, and Niqter. The conductor knew them very well. He tore the ticket before they got in and when he was on leave, his replacement tore the ticket as he too knew where these men were up to.

Their Soap spoke it all. They all smelled unique, according to the factory they worked. It was their life-saving smell, their smell, and the company's trademark. The men sat like robots in the assembly line; no smile, no Hi's, and no life. Just the blank expression that one wears during the funeral. The flies were independent to travel their skin in and out. The driver, who was posted in that area for ten long years was like a gravedigger, praying for the men to rest in peace while letting them get consumed by monsters in the factory.

It all started ten years ago. In 2070.

When the groundwater vanished, there was a huge deficit of drinking water, and the government sought to solve the problem by filtering saltwater from the ocean. The mechanism worked but with insurmountable costs. The energy consumed by the machines was unfathomable making it even more difficult to desalinate the water. Fossil fuels were exhausted, and the sunlight took the difficult to reach after getting absorbed by the carbon in the air.

The extracted salt went on mounting up, finding no use except to add it pinch by pinch into the weightless chicken soup. The leading corporations like Ozorol, Zista, and Canori pumped up with motivation proposed the government to privatize the water filter units, whose proposition won the majority votes in the senate.

With water in private hands, the taxes went high and the public reacted negatively. Thus came the system of Premium and Platinum membership.

'You need more water,' they proposed, ' buy our Premium Membership status. If you want unlimited water, buy Platinum Membership status. For the rest of you, we have silver membership. You work for our corporation in a factory near the beach, and we give you sufficient water to bathe and wash your vessels and clothes.'. Many agreed, some didn't. Those who didn't were forced to agree as they failed to rummage fresh water on their own. Kim was one of them. Having lost his mother at an early age, he stayed unmarried for the sake of his father who suffered from Kidney Stones. Ravinder was being treated in a local hospital under the care of Ozorol. He knew where the problem emerged, yet he could do nothing.

To ease the burden on a single corporation, the tender was given to all those who came forward setting up the greatest battle to prepare freshwater. The companies lacking employees went on to form some impressive campaigns throughout the country. With a population of trillions and jobs in millions, men agreed. Soon these companies introduced the Smelly Soap Formula to attract new baits. They said that their soap and its smell were unique, that it would clean a body with the least amount of water. The research to find the Productivity-increasing smell was done with more frenzy than towards purifying water. The world moved on, with the soaps competing with sweats and the people burning their lives for water.

The bus wheezed along the Salt Road, just aside from the beach, with factories in between, obstructing those dark polluted waters from the view. The plastic was being fished every day to feed the bacteria. The rebels, who frequently failed to loot the rich men's water lived on the shore. Their skin along with their aim to free the water decomposed every day by the rough climate and tough surveillance by these corporations.

Salt Road was the road where none except halophiles lived. The roadside looked like it was snowing salt. The tires powdered the salt and moved like a metal crusher. Instead of engine sound, the crush and smash of salt were dominating while the surrounding turned damp with the irritating smell of the factory outlet. Except for the replacing bus conductor, none of them felt reluctant towards this ghoulish environment. On the heap of salt stood huge billboards placed by these factors shaped corporations. Who were they advertising if no one was prepared to enter the Salt Road? Their customers were the workers at rival companies. There were a few who decided to come up with machines for human work, but no matter what metal they mixed and molded, the salt and the weather distorted their work making way for biological machines to fill their place.

We Pray and Pay for your Family....Join Us NOW and Get 10% extra water per day...Give a missed call to 34345 or text us at ozorol@care.com

No other place like Hynro...You are our Hero and We, your humble Maestro.

Join us NOW and get free unlimited water for a day in a month.

Give a missed call to 111111 or text us at Iamhero@hynro.com

The billboards never did end until the first company arrived. It was Niqter. The men wearing yellow shirts and brown pants got down taking with them, their smell of french perfume fumbling in an AC room. Next came, Hynro, the men wearing, white shirts and blue pants got down taking with them, the smell of daisies on the fresh field.

Sinqil and Canori went off to arrive at the Ozorol, the first company to be established and the biggest of all. The men had the smell of mud on the first rain. It had evolved with a mixture of paints, old books, and sweets. Anyone smelling it for the first time was doomed to experience the state of LSD without hallucinations.

Kim got down along with twenty other men, whom he never cared to get introduced. Kim's red skin attracted some unwanted attention. They looked at him in amazement. Although he worked in a salt dissolving department, the last job you would take, he very well knew that all that they did was throw away the salt on the road at midnight after filling it in a barrel. One easy way was to dump it back into the sea, but there was a problem. Their salt would reappear once again.

The government didn't interfere because, by that time, the government was composed of men from these companies. They were playing politics to favor their companies. It went to an extremity where each company has formed a political party demanding their workers to vote just for their leader.

Kim, wearing his second mask, with a huge astronaut-like suit with a glass helmet, that didn't let dampness suck his skin, walked towards the compression filters, where salt got separated. With a plastic shovel, he had to fill three barrels of salt before the end of his first shift. The work was hard and was specially made for men like Kim- strong with muscle and weak with his father's image in the hospital. The shovel went slippery, and the gloves and the leather boots were sweaty after two dumps into the barrel. He couldn't remove and blow the air because the salt was too concentric to touch. The dormitory room where workers slept to dream about Premium Membership was the only solace. Bursting through the salt, he made his way to meet his only friend.

The factory was posing its vastness to his giant posture challenging him and mocking his life to reconsider death. The workers looked like bacteria being experimented on in a culture. At least, those bacteria under human care were not aware of their state and fate. What is my purpose? Kim thought and tried to answer it at will. There was no power to formulate his own purpose with his thought process- it would fall heavily on his mind. Is it to die and get consumed like plastic? Or is it to find a way to fly like dust? There was no answer except questions to add to his purpose.

"There you are, Kimmy!" roared Rubik, flailing his fat brown hands out wide.

"Please No! Not Now!" Kim went past his open hands and grabbed the towel after removing his suit.

"Just a few more months you know, I will get fifty extra liters per day..." Rubik eyed Kim, who didn't seem to be interested, "Don't be jealous of me, I will let you have some, after all, we joined the factory together. Remember?"

Kim sighed, "Have you ever realized that your few more months have been happening for the past two years?"

Rubik's round face went dull. His expanded cheeks wrinkled with the loss of blood and his big mouth uttered some unknown words. His dark eyes looked at his pale feet, and his white hairs were vanishing from the top of his head.

"I have to go!" said Kim, and began rewiring the suit.

"Wait! You can't just go like that...Let's have a talk and see, will you? I am alone, you see, many of my men have given up on their dream and moved on to work in shifts."

"So!"

"I want you to join me here buddy."

"For fifty extra liters? You want me to work eighteen extra hours? It is inhumane."

Rubik looked into robotic-faced Kim. It was expressionless except while loathing the lifeless factory and its salt.

"Look where your inhumane philosophy took you to? If you had agreed to the manager's proposition and voted for Ozorol, you wouldn't be here."

Kim chuckled, "My life is already ruined. If they could see who voted for whom, what difference would it make now?"

Rubik's big fat body sighed, "But they clearly saw you stealing water with those rebels. Think about your father,"

"He's already dying anyway. Every time he drinks that low-class water, he ingests salt adding a quarry of stones to his kidney. Do you believe that our manager will provide pure water to our families? Well if you do. You are mistaken. And what's wrong with joining a revolution? Water is everyone's right. Those people did what we should be doing now, but here we are- afraid of losing water. They want us to survive, not live"

Rubik was used to it. Ever since Kim stopped working the extra shifts, he didn't take an extra chance to convince his friend.

"If you want to suffer, do it not in front of my eye. Trying to change the world by stealing someone's water won't change a bit. They will catch you and bury you in the salt. You're lucky that you found an alibi. Remember, I won't stand by your side again. Now go and fill those barrels."

Kim patted Rubik on his shoulder and walked back not forgetting to count his steps.

One must fill six barrels a day. If they miss, the water supply would be reduced. Kim, tired and weary got back on the bus to follow the routine for the next few months to see if the manager had the heart to change his fate with some inflation. The water was the currency and salt was the money burner.

The wig was shaggy and it fitted loosely on his head. The purple-colored dye was the last option and if the manager asks he was prepared to say while looking legit and smelling like model Ozorol man, 'I have been so busy working sir, that I have forgotten to cut them. And the color purple suggests that one is close to the art of doing things perfectly'..

The world seemed a messy place, not every time, only the time except he goes through the story of the natural pool. The reality was messy for Kim.

The careless bath, the bus, and the work. But, the manager was an addition for that day. He was the perfect man a woman desired for all her seven lives. The man with muscles stretching out of his fit shirt. Face- clean and manly with a dark mustache and low-cut beard. The eyes were as lively as a small child, shining and radiating perfection. Hairs tied at the back were so thick that they counted more than the combined hairs of men working in Ozorol. Nobody knew his name, they just called him Manager, who appeared every once in six months to check the status of a worker and grant-if he wish, some ways to make them burden-free.

Rubik was the first on the line. He held his report pressed to his chest as if he was hiding it from his fellow men. He limped at the standing place and bore a wide smile showing his yellowed teeth which he didn't take for embarrassment. Yellow teethed and hairless men were respected for their hard work.

"Rubik!" yelled Mr.Perfect sitting on his chair with a table, careless towards the men lined up till the end.

"Dear sir, dear sir. Am I glad to see you? So healthy, I pray God to give you many many years." Rubik made the best of himself.

The manager flushed with ecstasy. Kim observed and didn't plan for his praise.

"Your report looks good...Thirty tons every day, that accounts for Eighteen barrels?" he looked at Rubik getting nervous and shy, "That's great!"

Rubik's heart went up with acceleration. His anticipation for fifty extra liters was in front of his eyes.

"But!" the manager stopped short.

"Any problem sir?"

"You see Rubik, we at Ozorol respect you for your dedication...But this time, " the manager changed his expression turning calculative, "the pipelines are all getting weathered out. So, we are helpless to allot this budget to the repairs. And don't worry. I assure you that you will get at least fifteen extra liters per day. Rubik? Is that Okay? If not-"

"It's fine sir. I am more than alright with your offer."

"Yes, thank you...Next please!"

Rubik went saying to himself, if not! If not! what a dreary thing. Oh my god.

There were only a few rules for workers.

Do your work with loyalty.

Work hard till the salt from your sweat touches the salt on the ground.

Accept the reward, if not, get ready to see your family suffer from salty water.

These corporations were controlling the water supply and they knew what homes got what amount of water. The idea to change to another corporation was an option at peril. If one does so, they would find the same state but with a different fragrance.

When it was Kim's turn, the manager didn't lift his eye to look at him. He went through the report and signed it. As Kim was about to leave, a boy of ten to twelve years with a big cloak and baseball cap came running towards the manager. His countenance was healthy and sharp, unlike any other urchins. His bodily weight was more than many workers.

"Father! Father!" he said with abhorrence tapping his feet loudly.

"This place is garbage, you told me that you would take me to the natural swimming pool. The time is up. Look at my body, I am feeling scratchy. Come on..."

The manager didn't lose his calm. He took out his son's cap and brushed his hair.

"I will take you soon after we finish."

"But when?" the kid smashed the ground with a hard tap.

"Just give me ten minutes...Why don't you go to the car and turn on the AC? You can watch cartoons if you want."

"I am not a kid"

"Yes you are," an employee with a square face and bushy eyebrows said softly making a funny face to ease the kid.

The manager, when he rotated his face, had polarised all the wrath in the world. His eyes were not blinking and the report was torn. The next time, his report must contain the work of the past six months combined with the next six.

Kim was familiar with that incident when he had asked for extra water to bathe.

But now, he is not counting his steps as he walked back to work. The idea of the natural swimming pool has bored a flower directly from the root of the story. He squandered and replayed the kid's words in his mind.

The story is real! It is still there, somewhere out, I had to find it. He thought and if he had to find it, he had to chase the manager leaving his work risking the next day's water.

So he did. He tore his suit and tossed the helmet and reemerged with his pink and black uniform. The freedom was blooming and it came with a dearly cost.

The low-efficiency car powered by the salt battery washed through the salt and he ran behind. He would catch up till the salt road ends and after that, he had no idea. Luckily, a bicycle of some poor factory worker who couldn't afford a bus was lying flat with blown-out tires. With no other choice, he rode on it. The legs were stretching after years of exercise, the eyes were facing the dull wind with irritation, the fingers stuck to the handle while the nose became scratchy. He could either concentrate on his body or the car. His body was with him, but the car wouldn't, so he decided to ride with all his strength. He felt hope along with the wheels of the car. It was costly yet dearly to chase. He longed to stop, but the car emerging out of the salt road increased its speed. Kim was losing his breath, the people were surprised at a sweaty figure struggling on a punctured cycle. He couldn't care more or less.

If there were no traffic lights, he would have never caught it up. It rode through the streets that went out of the city. The car was smoke-free and soundless. The cycle was smoke-free too but the sound seemed sketchy to bring a heart attack to a passerby. The cars belonged to the top one percent with restricted use of Air Conditioner. The middle-class still rode their motorcycles struggling with their century-old ancestral desire to climb the ladder of wealth. The lower working class either used cycles or let themselves carried in public transport, and their aim to raise a communist government remained in the ideation stage. They all failed to get their share in eternal comfort and they all cursed the same thing again and again- their ancestors for not taking action on climate change.

It was at the final moment when Kim was giving up, that the car stopped.

They were out of the city. The street was empty, with a big torn building standing idly among the dry bushes and trees. The building looked like a Rome colosseum with a roof. It was big yet unattractive even for a dog to wait and consider moving in.

What kind of pool would there be? There was no sign of water around. Consumed by curiosity and hope of relieving his childhood story, Kim dropped the cycle in a bush and secretly walked towards the figures entering the building. The entrance was a small door with exposed bricks and the path inside went dark. Kim waited for some time to pass and as he pecked his eyes through a side window, it was dark again.

His only option was to move through the door. He came crawling on his knees and in the darkness, he could sense a smell that the manager left behind.

Slowly he moved in and when surrounded by the dark, his head stuck something woody. It was a table. He didn't express pain for it would be too costly.

"Who is there?" a coerce dry voice came out. "These damn cats! Shew! Shew!" The voice dropped and reemerged with a snore.

He followed the smell on his knees and after some twenty to thirty yards the sound of flowing water was heard. No way! He thought and the images of the pool came rushing in. He rose to his feet and walked flailing his hands to the front and after some hundred to two hundred steps the light emerged through the door.

It looked like Heaven's gate as if God was waiting to receive his disciple. He couldn't hold any longer. He drudged fast towards it and the sound became louder. Pleasant sound, birds, the swish of trees, the owl's hoot, the pigeon's cry, the crumbling of water, a splash of water, and the sound of spring breeze.

He had already begun to feel relaxed. His hairless eyebrows were raised, his mouth half open and chest heaving outward at every step. He rubbed his eyes before entering the light. It was in his last step when his eyes went uncomfortable. The bright light cocked his eyes like needles and he was near to screaming for his life.

He rubbed and rubbed and stood without shaking. His life was about to change and so it did.

The eyes slowly opened to expose nothing but broken walls and pillars trying their best to carry the pressure while getting housed by rats and cockroaches. The soil on the ground, dust flying around, and the century-old plastics getting slowly decomposed by the remaining bacteria. At the center of the hall was a huge glass-walled room with a kid-sized water pool embedded inside, leaving a small room gap for changing clothes and post swimming shower. From under the ground emerged two huge water pipes connected to the glass wall. Manufactured by Bathalive,-.the premium and platinum water provider

The boy and his father were in the water, sprinkling water at each other's faces, laughing with intent after watching each other get wet. Kim felt it whimsical. They were floating in a short-lived fantasy with the distorted world around them.

The kid stopped short from throwing water and rotated at this standing place, placing his hands on his head.

"Look father, a butterfly! Wow! It has so wonderful wings. Beautiful! Amazing! I can't believe what I am seeing." he exclaimed and surprisingly the kid was facing Kim.

He didn't react to this salt and sunburnt figure. He went on exclaiming the things he claimed to be seeing "The flowers from the tree...so filled with colors and so fresh. I can't wait to take them home father."

"No son!" the manager burst out as if he heard blasphemy, "You can't take or touch anything. Just see and enjoy. Seeing is feeling."

Kim moved to the glass door, the sound was coming from the speakers from the ceiling and under the pool. The glass walls were thick and Kim pressed it with his palm and felt the coolness from it. He pressed his cheek to it and was not ready to let go.

"Father! When will be come back here? I want to go near that sun setting in the valley"

"Next time kid," the manager laughed, and whispered aside "it's time we change the setting."

Kim looked with tears in his eyes and felt pity for the kid stuck in a simulation.

The steps approached drowsily from the door. Kim circled his way out through the empty hallways, and broken windows, passing along some dusted landscapes of beaches. He wanted to pause and grasp what a beautiful beach looked like. Better not! he thought, hopes are destined to bitter disappointment, and grabbed the cycle back to work with steady happiness.

We are all the same he thought, equally deluded with sufferings and solutions.

CHAPTER FIVE

ROGUE READER

She forgot! The characters, the plot, and even the theme of the novels she had read throughout her whole life had evaporated like a spilled acid from the time she woke up that day. "How can I forget everything?" Kiera asked herself again and again desperately glancing at her thousands of neatly arranged rows of books on a shelf stuck to every corner of the wall surrounding her. Her pointy nose was dull, her thick cheeks got shriveled and her wide mouth was struggling to find the right words. "I can remember the movie, and my favorite song still hymns, Why not my books?" she wondered grabbing her tight fist in between her teeth, feeling like she's stuck in the dire transition to death. Her slender face was bulging, and her tied brown her emerged out in layers of confusion.

Staying alone in the quiet street of Goa, Kiera a single middle-aged woman managing her lodge has left with no other option but to seek the help of her visitor, Dr.Ashwin, a psychiatrist as per his entry on the room register. "Should I seek his help? " she asked herself and with no prior confirmation Kiera rushed to Dr. Ashwin's room with the owner's key and sat on the bed showing propriety over her actions. Dr.Ashwin, a decent-looking man in his fifties, had a bulgy stomach that heaved and relaxed before she intruded his wondrous sleep. He was deep in his dreams before he woke up like a curious cat after feeling her breath tensing his facial muscles. He got melancholic and confused about all those developments around him. "Can I help you ?" he asked with mixed expressions of shock, fear, and lust. "Should I ask him? What if he thinks I have gone mad?" She asked herself and finally let her words go out with a shaky tone trembling at regular intervals "I don't know why?" she began " Suddenly, all the books that I have read... I just couldn't remember anything.". He looked at her expressions through confusion and stress and found that her words had no confidence left to show some alibi. Psychiatrists have a beautiful tendency to solve the problem by listening to the victim's story and by letting them know how they feel about it they ease their path toward a solution. He repeated the same trick "Very well, this sounds interesting" he began with a smile trying to comfort Kiera"Can you tell me what happened yesterday?" he asked and continued with a smile and sat with his back comforting on a pillow. "Should I tell him about the whole day? She questioned herself and tried to confirm it "You mean the whole day?" she asked raising her eyebrows. "Yes, the whole yesterday, if you are comfortable with it" the reply was soothing.

"Yesterday, I woke up and attended the reception and read a book until the afternoon. I ate some lunch and took an afternoon nap till evening and after having a cup of tea I continued with the book, when night fell I went to a nearby restaurant to have dinner and after returning I slept fine turning the pages of the incomplete book"

There was nothing strange in her story except her way of telling it, she raised her pitch every time she mentioned the word 'book' and got excited with it like it was the reason for this strange illness.

"Which book was that?" asked Dr.Ashwin trying to find out if there was some clue hidden inside it. Hearing that question, Kiera's anger seemed to rush out through her reddening face. "I said, I don't' remember anything" she shouted "Is he a psychiatrist" she doubted him and looked lost in her thoughts. "Can I visit your library?" The psychiatrist asked her in a soft tone with his unsure voice. He was already terrified by her changing behavior, but her insane story triggered him to visit her room for whose request she agreed without growing hard on him.

Dr.Arwin looked around to see nothing but books. Books of crime and history were given extra care with neat labeling with numbers. There were up to 365 crime novels and 366 history books and Dr.Ashwin wandered looking closely near all of them. The aroma of a sweet freshener stuck his nose. What the hell does he think he's doing? she asked herself looking at him getting lost in her world of books? Dr.Ashwin turned around to find nothing of importance that would lead him to suspect her behavior but behind the door he found an old calendar hanging with cross marks on some of the dates. "Why are you still having an old calendar?" he asked holding in his arms while sticking his eyes on her face. Listening to his question, her anger erupted again like a volcano. "Do you mind keeping it back?" she asked rashly. What is he? A psychiatrist or a detective? She wondered and went near her crime collection and began cleaning a clean shiny book. Dr.Ashwin was left with nothing to ask, and found no hope in curing her illness due to her haughty replies. He turned back and as he was about to leave the door, he saw a huge clock over the door stuck at 3.30. His will felt that there was no need for an inquiry about it, but his curiosity seemed to fail his willpower. "Why is the clock........"

"Enough" she screamed with all her might and when he turned back he saw Kiera standing straight with her legs intact, horror in her eyes, holding a gun facing straight to his forehead. Her anger lost its extreme potential and watching his sweaty sunken face Should I kill him now? She asked herself for the one last time and the next moment, the trigger met with the gun's body spilling blood all over her calendar. She continued with her angry face till she was satisfied with his blood-soaked head.

"Only I am allowed to ask questions to me" she declared and introduced a new book in the crime section equaling it to that of History.

CHAPTER SIX

MR.HEADLESS

Getting off the bus, rolling back his blue shirt sleeve over his hands, and wiping off the sweat over his forehead, Gru is all set for his first day at the job. His body trembled with excitement, mind boggled with numerous thoughts, blood pressure was unstable with the sight of a large building that stood like a titanic ship with a glass wall stretched out like a hull, and at the pointy edge stood a flag of pink color. 'Pink brings peace!' Gru said to himself and walked towards the entrance rummaging the ID card for his IT company-Synborg, from his bag.

His hand pecked inside the bag and shook unnecessarily. While wearing the card on his neck, a faint disfiguring thought occurred out of nowhere, 'Is it the end? Or the beginning?'. He had no patience to think it over. The people around him were doing all the same- getting inside the door like a pray being swallowed inside a snake's mouth. His thin brows furrowed, lips debunked and his face turned pale as he imagined himself as a fellow prisoner of responsibility. His brown eyeball was examining every step he took. The floor was clean and reflected his face daring him for a new life. His mother wished for this day, his father was watching him from heaven and his sister was ready to pay her dowry with his salary. The world was moving fast, taking everything, while leaving his problems behind. Problems are not time-bound, they play by their own rules and many a time defies logic. 'If everything goes as I expected' he thought, 'I will restart my painting...'. It was a promising thought, but the destiny of his present choice was yet to uncover the newness in him.

"The best way to win over a job and attain some promotion is to please the boss," a senior recruit had suggested during a briefing that took place two months ago. From then on, not a day went by, when Gru left off from the series of self-help books and productivity tips. He appeared confident to himself, but as always, his instinct was poor to cope with a new scenario. Unlike every other recruit, Gru found himself at a loss for something. Maybe it was a lack of smile, bent shoulders, or is it his fear of missing out? He couldn't know.

The security scanned his ID and pointed him to the lift that would take him to the second floor. Gru preferred stairs against a lift. He believed that an ill omen presided inside the lift. He was strengthened by the confirmation bias that said that 'lift marks laziness'.

The stairs were slippery but his new brown shoes were supporting his wide and long gait perfectly. His eyes scanned the images on the wall. They were certificates, medals, and images of people with suits and big names. One of the portraits was washed off with a face. The picture showed the body with a black suit, bow tie with no neck, and no head. He rubbed his eyes before moving on. He drank half the bottle of water and looked again. The face didn't seem to appear. It felt odd and scary. Below, at the corner was the name of the man without a face. Dr. Sham Shrikanth.

"What is happening here?" He whispered and the spit out of his mouth landed on the portrait. He rubbed it off immediately wishing to go invisible for a brief amount of time.

A man with a bulgy stomach and a gigantic spectacle with a golden frame, most likely the oldest and most experienced employee, was climbing the stairs like a trekker before him. He was counting his steps.

"34...35...36...37...38..." he sighed, and drew all the sweat in one swish, "Damm the steps. I should have taken the lift," he sighed again and climbed,

"37...38..."

"Excuse me! Sir!" Gru motioned his hand respectively. "You left at 38,"

"Stairs man!" said the fat man, "Stairs make me crazy and dumb. Thanks anyway...39...40-"

"Sir! May I know who is in the picture?" asked Gru, still maintaining the respect by keeping his legs closed and straight.

The fat man scanned Gru from top to bottom. Cocked his head, lifted his eyebrows, and widened his lips, "New recruit?" he asked humorously.

"Yes, I am..."

"Developer or Tester?"

"Developer,"

"It is better if you satisfy with this faceless image of your boss." the fat man approached Gru and laid his hand on his shoulder. It weighed more than a bucket full of water. Gru looked at him in bewilderment. The fat man laughed and continued, "Look, you will be adjusted to this...to be frank, no one has seen his real face."

Taking his hand off, the fat man walked to the second floor and settled on his spongy seat that was counting its last date.

Gru fastened his legs pushing aside the thoughts of Mr.Headless. The grand hall- his workhouse, was steps away. As he emerged through the door, he saw that the cubicles were arranged like roofless boxes in a maze. Every movement of his head revealed a man or a woman with a full blue shirt, holding a coffee mug and a laptop, walking briskly with tension on their faces, who had no moment of relaxation to acknowledge his presence. He expected some grand handshakes and hugs from his fellow colleagues, but the business of the workhouse appeared like a beehive. Work...work...work. He felt his hardest imaginations come true, and the headless boss's chamber that stood in the corner was stuck with newspapers on the glass wall. The door was slightly ajar and all the voices from the cubicles ended in the hall. Gru successfully scanned his nameplate placed over the cubicle corner- the only successful venture he was part of. He found a computer with an internet connection and the fat man he met on the stairs was a single chuckle away.

A file on his desk was filled with the day's work. They had assigned the work of 12 hours to be completed in 8 hours. Being well defined with handwork and determination, Gru was confident, I can do this in 6 hours, he said to himself.

"Hello, Sir!" Gru began, standing at the threshold of a fat man's cubicle. Robin, the nameplate said.

"Newbee!" Robin said, trying to take his eyes from the computer screen that ran enormous lines of code of small size that explained the size of his spectacles.

Gru smiled and said, "I am done,"

Robin looked at him in astonishment, "Done already? You just joined today...how can you think of leaving the"

"No No No...I am done with the day's work,"

Gru witnessed Rubin going through the change of a lifetime. Like a dry tree bearing colorful leaves. "Are you sure you are not playing with me? That's 12 hours of work, how can you finish it in less than 6 hours?"

Gru blushed, and stood straight for his answer, "I am used to it,"

Robin nodded and had no words to spit.

Gru, bending forward, carefully asked for permission to enter the cubicle by pointing his hand. There was no second chair in that cubicle and the files were struggling to bear the least of space given to them. The photograph of Robin along with his five-year-old daughter was pasted beside the monitor was being attacked by the raising pile of files.

"I was thinking of meeting the boss!" Gru said and eagerly waited to hear the reply.

Robin chuckled. It looked as if he was dealing with a fool. "Boss!?", he began to laugh. The kind of laugh the psychopaths show to kids to freak them out.

Gru turned uncomfortable, "What's wrong?"

"What's wrong? Nothing's wrong..." Robin looked relieved, " Look... I don't mean to demotivate you or something but listen...nobody here wants to see the boss, they work seriously and leave it to themselves. The serious faces around you are fake. They are acting to show it to the camera. The boss sees everything that happens outside of our cubicle "

Gru looked around and heard giggles and secret phone calls inside numerous cubicles. It felt real and stupid to witness something so bizarre to think about.

"So what about my work? I want to report it to him."

"You want to report? Do as you wish!" said Robin, turned back to his computer, shifted the tab that opened a shooting game, and began blasting bullets with his mouse, "If I were you... I would have chilled all day long after completing the work. Nobody cares, if you do it first or last. All that matters is that you do it," he became mute with huge headphones on.

Gru grew curious and set his foot towards the boss's chamber.

Somewhere in his mind, Mr.Headless's head began to take shape. He tried to join the attributes with the extreme sense of imagination. The eyes moved throughout the face, lips were stretched across the ears, the nose protruded like a beak and the boss appeared like a disfigured great man with epilepsy.

As he moved towards the plastered chamber, he sensed that some fifty to a hundred pairs of eyes were watching him play the game of death. His breathing only got denser, and the sound of his heartbeat overtook the clickety-click of his shoes. The world around him was censoring the man with a wit to meet his headless boss. He wanted to turn around, but couldn't. He wanted to run away, but he was already on the verge of his destination. What would happen the most? He asked himself, will he cut my throat? Impossible! I have always been a good athlete. I can survive this.

The glass door handle to the boss's chamber was cold with a drizzle of cold air from the air conditioner. As he peeked, the fading smell of rotten meat blasted on his face forcing him to reconsider the course of action. Unconsciously, his legs filled the room while he was still in a blank slate of the smell. The eyes opened with the distinct surprise that one gives while watching a lizard hunt a fly. The room was clean with no files, the nameplate was missing, the computer screen was transparent with an open desktop, and the paperweight was made of glass with a head of a man with pig's face like the poster on Orwell's Animal Farm. Under it, a white paper reflected saying, There is a possibility.

What does that mean? Gru asked himself.

The chair in front of the table was turned away. A man was seated, showing the back of his head to Gru. His hair was neatly cropped and the color of the suit was that on the poster. In Front of him was a big screen split into rows and columns of live camera footage. The head glared at it with unseen eyes.

The chair didn't seem to shake and the fan added an extra length of coldness while there were many unsealed packets of sugar snap peas, carrot, cucumber, and berries. They were nutritiously rich. Gru gulped the empty spit through his throat.

"Sir!" Gru whispered loudly, filled with unknown fear.

There was no reply, "Hello Sir!" he whispered again.

"I finished my day's work!" he exclaimed in confidence and was disappointed without an answer.

"Excuse me, sir!"

No reply.

"Hello sir, I am Gru, a new recruit, I have heard a lot about you."

No reply.

Gru's temper was short-lived, the innocence in his words was faltered and his face became brisk with impatience.

"Can I get a reply?"

No reply.

"Am I disturbing you? Sir...Is it true that no one has seen your face?"

No reply.

The file in Gru's hand slipped off his hands and fell on his feet. He bent down cursing Mr. Headless within himself. The eyes, red with anger while looking down took the sight of the boss's legs from under the table.

He was shocked and laughter was at the threshold. There were no pants on his legs. The tissue papers were spread across the ground. The junky saliva was all around making it messy as hell.

Is he alive? Asked Gru why doesn't he talk?

"Sir!" he said loudly, and his voice was distributed out of the chamber to all his colleagues.

No reply.

He turned around, frustrated, and headed back to his cubicle. He sat looking bluntly into his computer.

"Did you meet him?" came the voice of Robin from behind. He was already smiling.

Gru shook his head in disgust.

Robin looked spookily, "If you really want to see his face! Report to him without your work."

Gru was taken aback. There's no way that he would withdraw from his work, I will finish my work much quicker and report, he became determined.

The same thing followed the next day. No reply.

Gru waited after office hours at least to have a handshake. Except for the courier deliverer- delivering food and tissues, nothing got in and out of the chamber.

Things began to appear mysterious. The boss was like a Dracula hiding inside his chamber afraid of the light from his employee's faces. The co-workers were all chilled out about it but Gru was not giving up on his quest..

After a week, the same steps marched towards the sealed chamber with a single difference. The file was incomplete to report.

Dark circles surrounded Gru's eyes and yesterday's sleep was calling him to rest. The past few days were hard with numerous assumptions about the possible futures. Gru, unlike others, always wondered about the extreme possibilities towards the effects of his actions. Will they remove me from the job if I didn't complete my work? He thought and the thought didn't seem to hold back his decision to confront the boss.

The door handle was cool, the smell of rotten mean fluxed out through the door. The chair was turned around and the screen was filled with office frenzy.

"Sir!" trembled Gru and felt staggering before speaking his next words. He cleared his throat, erected his chest, and spoke, gathering all the strength he had, "I am sorry that I failed to complete my work." he began to let out a deep sigh, that's when the chair tilted left and right. Gru checked himself, confirming his position in between the weird chamber, and looked back. The door was closed, the fan ran with frenzy and the ac went higher and higher passing cold chills making him shake and turn desperate for warmth.

Gru watched the head with intent. With the passing of every minute, the back of the head appeared bulging with flesh. The black hairs were growing and the shoulders appeared rising with mass. Somewhere in his mind, Gru noted that the figure was shifting into something he knew.

"What did you say?" the voice bumbled with the mix of machine and human. It was sore and devilish.

"I..." staggered Gru, losing his wits, "am sorry, sir... I didn't complete my work."

The tilting chair began to move with some added frequency. The voice was absent and within a fraction of a second, the chair rotated with the figure sitting erect without disturbance.

Gru stumbled with loss of breadth looking at the face.

How is it possible? He wondered with a horror-stricken face. This shouldn't be,

The man on the seat. The boss. The mystery- was revealed.

It was Gru himself.

Gru flailed his hands and drew backward and reached for the door. He turned the knob and ran outside. The eyes were lined up to see him explode out of the chamber.

Robin was sitting quietly and Gru ran before him.

"Do you know what I saw?" he asked.

"I know." Robin replied," You saw me there."

CHAPTER SEVEN

The Kangaroo

We, the Kangaroos are well known for hopping upfront leaving a considerable amount of land untouched as if the part of the land our feet meet is meant to be derived from special soil. One might sarcastically reason to debunk our unique movement by saying that we resemble a frog in doing so, but here is my retortion to that unsettling opinion, a frog is dirty and sticky and unbearable with its ugly skin- humans shy away from its presence. A frog is small too, and the way we carry our babies in our magnificent pouch is unimaginable on the scale of comparison that one tends to make here, it just doesn't fit in. I am not boasting myself as a superior race of animals or an animal with divine powers derived from our mother nature. We breed, they do too. We eat, they do too. We survive and they do what it takes to live. Removing these inherent characters ordained by nature on us, we resemble frogs on yet another condition. We both can't hop backward. Is that the problem of not having an extra pair of eyes on the back of our heads? Years ago, when I was a feeble two-year-old joey, I thought it through, and the answer seemed too tough to approach with formal reasoning. Elephants could walk backward. Lions could, tigers could, and interestingly some fishes could swim against their sneaky forward motion too. So, where is this leading? I thought and was determined to try all the available options at my disposal. Of course, I didn't cross my ambitious thoughts against the physical barrier by assuming myself of growing wings to fly against the tornado or flexing my body with numerous colors to hide against the attack of foxes. I wanted to try what others could't even though they could. It was not a sudden uprising of non-conformity but was merely an act of curiosity. To sum it up, "Maybe I could hop backward!".

The light was getting eaten by the darkness in the sky. The sun, craftily consumed by the mountains on the horizon, was being greeted by birds of myriad colors that shouted the ending of a day in their own voice of irritation and splendor. The nocturnal's were craving out of their homes, after sleeping for the day all. When I woke up that day, the shade of the tree I was part of had merged with the never-ending land. Maybe it was the wind with the aroma of damp mud or maybe it was my unparalleled excitement after seeing a spider weaving its web around a dead insect, I was determined with my heart and spirit to hop backward. I wanted to feel like going back. I wanted to show my quirkiness and become the first kangaroo to move backward. Before doing so, I had a deduction to clear my way.

The rest of the kangaroos with me were ready to explore the pre-explored land, playing the game of stand-on-tail, eat-the-meat, and drown-the-tiny-enemy. The mob, which I followed lazily carrying heavy steps and unemotional face, was too unstable to stand still in a certain place and look at the sky and wonder what would it take to reach the stars. I wondered what made them so volatile. Small me, trying to calibrate their un-understanding navigation was soo dumbfounded as the fact got revealed by my mother.

"It is the alpha male..." she said, suppressing her lustful desire towards him, "He calls all the action.". Then I asked her if I could be spared with some time, unassailed by the mob, at least for a day?

Her face, tranquil until then, exhibited the expression of watching a sin being committed. She took a small jump against me, brought her face toward mine, "Die!...You will Die if you stay away!" she screamed, and the air of her mouth, brushed my face like a rough rock.

There was no use talking to my mother. Her answer ended my exploration before it began. Death, she had reasoned would be the final feedback of my attempt. Scratches and tiny cracks seemed to take forms, little by little, on the vacant road of my dreams. I spent that night with the mob. My mother keenly kept her stern eye on my body, looking backward as if I was conspiring to kill the alpha. The rest of the gang didn't acknowledge my presence except to call on for a fight which I denied straight away. They were delusional, carrying a burden, to become the one like the alpha and rule the mob twisting our path with their changing thoughts. I felt left out by my surroundings and my mind was relentlessly accompanying me by making sense of what I felt was not actually weird. By the daybreak, I didn't sleep but kept my eyes fixed on the line of ants that followed through my toes, sneaking like air, unaffected by the warmth of my body. I forced myself to watch their hairlike legs, which moved with so swift an action that no matter how much I focused, went unseen. Through the strain rolled down my tears, beads like, silvery, glistening against the morning sun, thick and spherical, falling on the line of ants, flooding their movement with an impact of a fireball. Two of the ants lay dead in front of me. I blew air out of my mouth to bring them back to their life. No effect, but the disjoint line of ants continued as if nothing had happened. There was no mourning. Death meant nothing to them. Does that instinct follow us? Hey! I heard my mob members die from insufficient food, from aggressive attacks from foxes and humans, but none...None was reported to be dead by hopping backward. And all of our dead mates were left behind as if they belonged to the mud and microbes they lay on. Every time a Joey is born, we tend to reframe our minds by convincing ourselves that we remain the same number since the beginning of time. The death was fooling us from hiding its face. On the other hand, my mother didn't, at first, know what it means to hop backward. If it brings death, so be it. At least I would be known to have died from hopping backward.

Every second passed like an eternity. I imagined my first backward hop on flat land, away from others of my kind, parrot floating overhead, guiding with the flutter of its wings, squirrels around me squeaking my wrong takeoff, and the wind feeding me the fading hope. My thoughts raced like unregulated dry leaves caught in a turbulent flow. Each took their own turn and many were stuck halfway through afraid of unexpected pitfall that could smash it into dust. I woke up in the afternoon to see that the sun was acting strange with extra rigor. The intensity of its flash was too strong and exhilarating for my tender eyes to see. I recuperated my eyeballs after brushing my face against the ground. It gave me some comfort. As I stood upright, amid the mob that slept like dead bodies, I had a vague feeling of betrayal. Was I becoming something else? Is it me who is trying to shame my kind because of my childish desire? It was tough to answer... and the more I thought, the more I fell in a loop of unending questions and answers. The design of every question in the world is such that, it can either relieve us from deeper delusion or leave us lurking behind the same story in search of perfection. I had no maturity to consider or get trapped in both of these scenarios. I had to try on action instead of quarreling with myself.

The time seemed perfect and something done unseen by peers goes unseen as if it has never happened. I slowly hopped away from the mob and reached a secure place surrounded by lush green trees like a giant natural cage. The ground was smooth with thick grass and tiny rocks that didn't affect my foot. The sunlight did rarely attempt to cause any harm as it was stranded by leaves like a roof of a human house. I began to worry and my eyes ceaselessly scanned for hidden attackers. My ears were erect as ever and my chest heaved as if my heart was bursting out to enjoy its freedom. Every little motion of a nearby leaf sent me into a frenzy. I leaped behind the tree as a twig was twirled by an innocent snake climbing the branch. I jumped high up on the ground to come to the same stand as a rat scurried unaware along my side. I tried to be calm but couldn't. It was no more an act of curiosity. It was becoming the test of my life. I felt I was becoming me with every inch of increased fear.

What use is there to hop backward? I asked myself, still scanning the surrounding. Does it help me in gathering food? Or does it make an alpha male? Or does it make others remember me for eternity? One thing was for sure. What others think, I couldn't guess and even if I did, I would be more wrong than right. Again, asking these questions and answering them has got me nowhere to the land of stress. I didn't care and finally made up my mind to hop backward once and get out of there.

As I focused my attention on my body, I found that everything I did from breathing and shaking my head to jumping and kicking my legs, I wasn't actually in control. It was as if someone else from the outside was moving me like a puppet. I realized that I had to recalibrate my body according to my wishes before taking a leap of my dreams. I shook my head and before I knew it, it shook without my awareness. I took a taste of my dry mouth. It was void and undisturbed by my tongue. It was time to the same thing with a backward hop. I drew a huge breath and before it all went out, I was jumping against my normal motion and before I felt a crying excitement, I was in the air, instead of hopping, I was jerking against the ground. I realized that I had a strong and thick tail that is constricting my backward motion strictly holding the ground. If my body isn't built to sustain a backward motion, maybe it's wrong to do it. I don't know why but this thought didn't occur to me. I tried again, this time, I carefully concentrated on my tail to lift it as I jumped. The air goes in my lungs, my legs get their extra share of blood, and up goes the body and falls back to the same position. The tail was stopping me again. The third time, I thought I had figured it out. I stood on a round rock, the height of my forward limbs from the ground. As I jumped backward, my legs didn't even reach the ground. My tail took the whole weight of my body and kept me balanced in the air like a root of a tree. The rock which was a part of my jump rolled forward against the force of my retreat from its surface and took on a flurry of noise as it went smashing against another. I immediately disengaged from that place and found my unfriendly refuge among the mob.

That day, there was some solace in the rest. I laughed at myself, chuckled and grinned, and felt the layer of unknown energy over the skin of my body. I did something new. Something that if I told someone, would never believe. I felt like I was one among the crazy clouds. Seen by everyone, touched by the wind, yet none could discern that it was a cause of thunder and lightning. I felt confident to try the same on the next day, but with better ideas and tricks to control my tail.

As I lay asleep in the evening, the mob was activated and was ready to find their peace of food. A joey, just like me, but of weaker body and thick fur, tapped its tail on my face. I woke up to find myself not ready for any activity. I heard the alpha growl and the mob simply followed him without a second thought.

"Maybe, you shouldn't have gone there," the joey said timidly his eyes on my tail.

I became aware of my drama among the trees. It was not far away in my memory as if fell like a huge rock on my head. I regained my strength in anxiety, got up, and followed the mob along with the spy.

"What are you talking about?" I asked, curiously, as if I never knew what he was saying. I failed halfway through containing my curious face. I knew I was in trouble if he spoke of it to someone. I waited for him to speak.

"I want to play that game," the joey replied, "Jumping back... and I can call my mother and brother too,"

I stood and stared at him with disbelief. Is that what he thought of it? A game?

"What made you think that I was playing a game?" I asked unaware that I gave up on the secret..

"I don't know, but it seemed fun to watch. And why were you playing alone? It's the first of its kind."

We continued hopping and maybe, I thought, he was not that smart. So, I rolled dice with his own contemplation.

"It's not a game to tell everyone about...It's a special one...It must be kept secret if you want to win."

The joey nodded and gave a bright smile.

"Should we play tomorrow?" he asked again, unable to control his enthusiasm.

"Of course!" I said, and warned seriously, "And if you tell anyone you will be dismissed from playing it."

The next afternoon, the sun was the same. Along with draining the water from my body, it had also sucked the memory of the joey who was about to join me. He lay asleep as I moved to my spot of practice. I remembered him only after the trees shed their aura of peace around me. I quickly became present, discarded from the weariness of lost sleep. I drew a long breath and caught the smell of the tree trunk's cork. It smelled luxurious and kept my neck straight due to its ample availability. I wanted it all before beginning my task.

The world was vast and my aim was small but the way to reach it overlapped the world. I spent more time than the quarter-the-sky movement of the sun from top to horizon. My tail didn't comply with my effort. It was attached to me like a rock. The lower part that jerked against the ground became lucidly hurt with rashes and inkling of blood. It became pain and yet I continued without a hiss or a growl. By evening, I gave up for the day and as I turned around, I saw the young joey. He stood amid two trees, behind him a huge rock raised overhead, giving a spooky smile, tapping his feet rhythmically, unblinking, observing me with utter delight. I wanted to explain my mistreatment to miss his call, but he was there with a surprise. The moment he stopped tapping his feet, the mob emerged behind him. The alpha male took over the rock and stood there with its stern face, as crooked as a crocodile's mouth. His hard chest, structured muscles over legs, and sheer eyes doubled mine in size. Those around the traitor looked at me in visible hatred as if their enemy was caught to be butchered. My mother didn't utter a word. She stood with her face masked with hostility. I was helpless.

That day, the day of my banishment, the day of revoke falls short from my enumeration against its profound impact that is carried till the present. The alpha, raising his chest against the ray of light, sinking with utmost pride and terror looked at me as an intriguing competition. Although I was small, young, and brittle against his stout physique, he straightaway challenged me for a duel. My heart sank to the ground, my legs trembled, my heart raced against the flow of time, body ran through a series of shivers weakening my every breath that fell short of reaching my lungs. I felt suffocated, my stomach didn't nourish my dry spit as it retraced back to my mouth. I bent my head and tried to symbolize my defeat before my blood tastes the ground.

"He accepts defeat!" announced a feminine voice from behind. Nobody knew the owner of the voice except me. It was my mother obscured within the female members afraid of her opinion getting recognized. I felt sorry for her. I kneeled to the ground to support her claim and the alpha laughingly accepted, but he had other plans too.

"You..." he shouted like a hungry beast towards me, "the mad, the unimpaired, and the foolish joey, for going against the norms of our community just to fulfill your selfish desire to hop backward will be banished from my mob. Your call towards protection against any hindrance will go unanswered as you are no longer a sane animal we wish to bear the responsibility towards. You are no longer a

Kangaroo. You will live alone and those who try to avail him by any means will be banished as well.", the mob responded to this thunderous announcement with a careful sigh. They saw me as an example of ruin. I kept my head hung low and didn't dare to see around until the air lost its thickness. I didn't know how to feel. Should I feel alienated? It wasn't new for me. Should I feel relief? Partly, Yes for the freedom I was delivered and No, for taking away my identity as a Kangaroo.

The surrounding, the old practice place, appeared new to me. It was calling me by a different name, a name I couldn't clearly grasp with my timid understanding. After the mob left, I had nowhere to go. The freedom came with an explicit cost. The cost of being self-reliant.

There came a day when I couldn't find the food. Then there was a day when I was cruelly frightened by my mob with their frigid noise. I meant to stay away from them, but they were hung to my back with an invisible thread. My residence under a short Eucalyptus tree was carefully intruded as the kangaroo's destroyed its bark and spread spikes all around the resting place. I had to clear my ground every day before calling in for a rest. They relentlessly spied me, watched me practice hopping backward as it was the only thing left for me to perform to clear my mind from unparalleled questions of sanity. My tail was tearing apart. The bodily rest ended up in agony. Every time I closed my eyes, there was fear of attack that lynched my mind from further sleep. Apart from the mob, the foxes were populating the area, their horrendous howl spread across the forest sent squirrels and rats rumbling for new adobe. The mob too became alert and the weight of their dependence increased on the alpha every passing day. Unknowingly, I was maintaining my proximity with the mob and I was really afraid.

The backward hop seemed hopeless like a caterpillar's immediate metamorphosis, after repeated falls. The mob openly laughed from afar. Apart from grazing, they employed extra time to watch me fail. I was the only joker in the arena of reckless spectators. My tail was degenerating and my heels were sweating blood and then the judgment day came passing by.

It was early morning when the sun was still covered behind the dark curtain. The long-forgotten humans arrived on the magical lifeless animal that carried them on its round legs, while profusing smoke from behind. Their unexposed bare skin always lent them an unconscious superiority among us. They appeared to be enjoying the forest when their white glaring face ruminated along with exposed teeth. Each of their forelegs, attached to their shoulders were carrying yet another magical creature whose sole aim was to watch us and remember what we do. They seemed more careful about it than the carrying animal.

The mob always got excited when humans arrived, while some ran with fear, some watched them, struck with a lightning bolt, unmoved, and unconscious of their present state and if triggered, ready to attack with their life. I stood aside from the mob in the empty land with thin grass surrounded by thick bushes that obstructed a normal vision from seeing behind. As I was separated loner, most of the human's eyes were curiously transfixed on mine. I could see them make comments, form hypotheses, and debate with each other for my sake. The alpha male from another side, who observing their dissipating attention toward him called in for action. He wanted me out of the ground and I barely noticed his attitude until he arrived towards me in just a few hops that took the humans with inspiring awe.

They cheered as he arrived towards me. I was ready to escape when the Alpha with a thick growl stopped me from disappearing around the bush.

"Let's duel!" he announced with his haughty face.

I shook my head in unbearable force, and said surrendering, "I don't want to,"

He looked back at the humans and found that he was on focus. "I don't care what you want, all I want is a Duel or get ready to die,"

I shook my head again, "I apologize if I had done anything wrong,"

The alpha was triggered with impatience, he took a deep sniff and began punching his chest with aggression. I moved away towards the bush in fear of a surprise kick that would disassemble my body parts. His rage only escalated and he followed me and we were facing each other. To my right at my body's length was a bush and far against it were humans with an unforeseen expression saying what-happens-next with jittering teeth.

My eyes met the alpha's, his breath struck my face, his pumped-up chest cleaved into finely structured armor and when his impatience with my disapproval for a fight took over his temper, his action against mine was conjured by a howl and a hush from the bush. Two pairs of foxes with leaking mouths jumped into the scene of action like surprise visitors. Their teeth glowered with the stain of thirst, their eyes transfixed on prey made no mistake to glance otherwise. Their front legs, stretched wide apart had formed an invisible momentum for them to take off while their thick body humbled for our blood to soak in. My wildest fears came close, I feared death for the first time, no matter how I reasoned it before- as unimpactful, it was all over my body like an extra layer of skin. I had to escape death.

The alpha felt the same as mine, but I knew he had some powers to expel before thinking of escaping. His attention on the foxes and his brief angry growl initiated the fight. He jumped against a pair of them and one got kicked on the face while the other escaping the leg was over his giant body. All I remembered before my magic movement was that his throat was hooked to its mouth.

The pair of foxes in front of me stood side by side with ultimate terror. They looked at each other and they took a step forward. Before I turn around they were preparing their body for a jump. I don't know how it happened, but, all I know is why it happened. I was hopping backward because my life depended on it. My tail stood in the free space like yet another nimble hair from my body. I carried my body with ease and when the situation preferred I rested my body over the tail and gave a kick on each of the foxes. It was successful and my excitement with my backward hop added extra courage to my push of punch through my leg. It became no longer a life or death situation, it was a happy movement filled with playthings. I ended the battle by reigning over all the foxes who ran away, harmed and bleeding through the nose.

Much to my astonishment, I was finally praised, along with my own mob, who saw from hiding, the humans from far away were as ecstatic as a misty mountain, the snow of uniqueness was falling heavily on their bodies. They soon disappeared and from then on, they kept on returning, just to watch me lead my mob. I have made it my life's aim to teach the younglings how to be ready for a backward hop not just for momentary protection, but for the planned attack on our oppressors. They love my teachings and the change that is raising them on a step of Kangaroo evolution. They believe that kangaroos are going to rule the world with a backward hop.

Then one day, when the midday was flaming hot and the stream of water comforted us with sprinkle sound from the top ear, I was captured by the humans.

The ones who saw me as a symbol of change kept me in chains inside a cage and were transported by the gas-emitting animal to their world. I saw their faces, actions, abode, and finally, their ambition when my cage was pushed inside a huge dark hall that held many more cages than mine. I can still voices of animals echoing through the wall like unleashed ghosts. A roar, the caw, the moo, the howl, the growl, the quack, the grunt, the squeak, the chatter, the bark, the meo, the bleat, the scream, etc Beside my cage was a frog croaking inside a tiny prison. I took my head toward his prison and asked, "Why are we here? And What are they going to do to us?" in a trembling tone. He answered me in a clear depressing voice, "I don't know but I had just begun on hop backward when this arrest happened".

I knew where it was going and there's no way out.

CHAPTER EIGHT

THE RAT

The scorching afternoon sunlight struggled to reach the ground. The trees with spikey leaves arranged in layers from dead yellow to lush green attached on shoulder-like branches hovering one over the others stood like brothers in a family photograph. The speck of ray that reached the ground after the enormous struggle was in for a disappointment. The smell and touch of the ground it so longed to witness were continually interrupted by Rats on a rampage over a dispute; a nut has been stolen from a burrow. On one of the trees, a Monkey, dangling upside down, after a day's hunt for food, watched as the scene took place.

The victim, a Black rat with strong legs and impressive manuevarablity over land and tree cried for justice from the possible suspects- the White and Brown rat.

"Who else could it be? Both of your burrows are just a scratch-on-mud, away from mine. We all could hear each other talk and breath from our burrows" the Black rat began pleading its case, circling the other two rats with contempt, "It has been happening from my ancestral age. We were deprived of worms crawling towards our territories, but now- nuts? How dare you take my belongings? I want justice and I don't care what it takes to get justice."

The White rat, silently sniffing the ground, thinking of ways to accuse the Brown rat, balancing his bulgy stomach, lifted its head to speak, "I know what you are asking for..." it said, faking compassion with keen eyes, "But, tell me Black rat. As per our ancestral records, is it not us, who helped you build your burrow so magnificently? Is it not us, who taught you to hunt insects on trees and ground? Is it not us, the White rats, who gave you nuts when your burrow was filled with mud-water during floods?"

The Black rat slowed down and scratched its head, thinking, but failed to grasp the past intoned by the White rat. "It may be...but..." it couldn't find any new evidence to falsify the White rat, and continued circling.

The Brown rat, silent until then, didn't intend to speak at all, but when it realized that both the other rats were waiting to hear it by casting a strict glance, resentfully, it shook its head and slowly grew up with its inherent unattractive voice, it asked Black rat. "I don't understand what your problem is?"

"A nut from my burrow is stolen", the Black rat shrilled and the White rat smiled nodding as if taking side with the Black rat.

"Just a nut right?" shrugged the Brown rat, "I don't think that there was a need to call in for a meeting for such a minor issue. If you would have come to my burrow, I would have given you a nut in the name of friendship."

The monkey on the tree was soon accompanied by a crow, whose smelly beak and dusty feathers disturbed the monkey to dangle freely from the branch.

"What is going on?" it asked in an enthusiastic craw. The Monkey, with no interest to pursue the conversation shrugged off with a wave of its hand.

"What is going on?" asked the crow again, now growing closer to the Monkey. The Monkey, unable to tolerate its smell said in an ignorant tone, "The Black rat's nut is stolen."

"Who stole it?" the Crow turned excited and examined the rats, " Is it the White rat, or the Brown rat? I believe it's the Brown rat...I mean, just look at the White rat? Isn't it pretty and fat already to steal from someone else's nut? I got to tell this to everyone in the forest."

Before it flapped its wings to lift its hollow body to the air, the White Rat, began.

"'In the name of friendship', he says" clearly mocking the Brown rat, carrying a narrow smile of sneakiness, "Then ask him, my dear friend...Where were his ancestors while your burrow was flooded?"

The crow, acquired with this new non-contextual information, cried to the monkey before flying away, "Did you hear that? The Brown rats are traitors. The world needs to know this. I better get going, otherwise, I may forget this special piece of information.'"

The Monkey didn't interfere, and neither did it care. It kept on dangling, looking upside down enjoying the unmoderated trial.

The Brown rat stood on its two legs, and defended itself by saying, "That's not the issue at hand, and, by the way, we had our burrows flooded too."

The Black rat nodded, convinced of the Brown rat's innocence. The White rat disturbed by the Black rat's confirmation, immediately shot back, "That may be true, Brown rat, and what about the time when you borrowed fresh nuts from us, only to return the decayed ones? Isn't that worth mentioning here?"

The patience of Brown rats has reached its limits. Before it crossed to violent temper, it breathed a huge air for comfort and spoke softly, still with an ill unimpressive voice, "Still, I don't see its relevance here. What has happened, has happened. We can't travel through time to change the way it happened. Why aren't we talking about the stolen nut anymore?"

Unaware of all the three rats, the animals from the forest were gradually gathering around the scene. The crow was quite successful in gaining attention for an unknown issue. The snake crawled around the trunk of the tree where the money was dangling. The deers settled beside the bushes, eating the grass as they wished. The Lion and its cubs took the shelter of the rocks that rose like cliffs near the scene. The Elephant, carrying raccoons over its back stood with an air of authority. The birds covered the branches like leaves. The insects were all around the ground, some peeking out of the soil and some protruding out of the tree trunks, and some resting on animal furs. It was a place worth noting. It had become a fight concert with a sufficient audience to cheer on each side. Unfortunately, they were crafted in with a bias.

Looking at the gathering, the White rat flushed with unknown energy, the luxurious of the three, spoke with its loudest voice, "Welcome my dear friends!" it said and before it corrected its failing voice a shrieking meo of the wild cat came rushing through the ears of all the gathered animals. It said, "We know it all. It's the Brown cat's doing. His ancestors didn't help the Black cats during floods."

"That's right" the White rat announced immediately. The Black rat nodded. The Brown rat, calling in for a calm discussion said, "But, we were in floods too. How can we help if we can't help ourselves? And, why are we talking about our past? It doesn't relate to what is going on in here right now."

The animals went silent. The Tiger, however, just arrived, jumped right into the scene, and furiously looked at the Brown rat, clenching its teeth and pressing the ground with its huge paws, tightly crushing the folds of mud into thin dust. "Your ancestors didn't help them during floods," it said, whose voice sent a cold chill in the heart of Brown rat. "Accept it, or die?"

"I accept," the Brown rat helplessly announced. "But...the issue is about a stolen nut."

The Tiger backed, proud of its achievement, and the animals bid their respect to this valorous act instead of paying attention to the Brown rat.

The White rat coming forward said in a glamorous tone, "My dear friends. I am so glad that you are all here...But this issue can't be resolved at once. May we take a leave for today? I am hungry, so might you be and the food is luxurious these days...We will continue this until justice arrives without bias."

The next day, the Monkey watched the animals gather one by one, taking their seats with their food ready to eat. The animals that were alone yesterday were arriving in groups. The crow, in spreading the news with its vast network, was so successful that the crocodiles from the faraway river took their interest for the unlikely trial. The fishes too were no exception. The storks carried them in their beak filled with water.

But, there was a catch on the scene. In front of the rats stood a white Rabbit, which had a reputation of understanding animal psychology,

"We don't need fights in our forest," it said and gestured at all the three rats, out of which, the Brown rat nodded with approval. “Fights end with violence. Let’s come to an agreement for once and end this without making it a bigger issue.”

The crocodiles, dire and dissatisfied with this verdict, crawled forward and said, “And who are you to settle this? I came to see them fight and I won’t leave until I see what I want. First of all, Brown rat’s ancestors didn’t help the Black rat’s ancestors during floods”

A murmur of yes’s and hoo’s went around and settled to nothingness.

The rabbit, taking steps away from the crocodile, ears erect and nose ready to detect the ambush, said calmly, “I am merely trying to maintain peace in the forest by stopping this fight. Someone stole Black rat’s nut and I am only encouraging them to converge towards an agreement. This small issue, need not be dragged and all of you might have better things to do than come here and waste your time.”

The crocodile laughed, whose open mouth exposing the savage teeth and stains of last prey, came haunting Rabbit. “So, you are trying to save Brown rat from possible punishment?”

“I never said that. And What makes you think I am on the side of Brown rat? In fact, nobody here knows who stole the nut.”

“But, it’s evident that the Brown rat’s ancestors didn’t help the needy Black rat’s ancestors during floods.”

The Rabbit, finally, losing the fear, took a step forward, “Where is the evidence?”

These words by Rabbit raised everyone’s eyebrows, the snaked hissed with confusion, the deers looked without blinking, the Lion dug the ground, and the monkey dangled with a sigh- still unchanged.

The crocodile, feeling a sense of shame in front of everyone, looking left and right, asked Rabbit, “Where is the evidence, that says otherwise?” it asked. “On the other hand, I have heard that yesterday, that the likely culprit, Brown rat confided of its ancestor’s crime in front of Tiger.”

The Lion, stopping the digging, jumped and nodded to everyone.

The Rabbit, eyed by the crocodile in a crude way, sensed a threat. “It doesn’t matter right?” it asked in a tone of defeat.

“Animal like you stand in the way of justice.” the crocodile said, licking its tongue to clean its teeth. The Rabbit was surrounded. Behind it was a jackal, left and right was adhered by a Tiger and a Leopard and the crocodile, walked forward hunched its body in vicious fury that its blood splattered all around the ground.

“We better continue tomorrow. It’s all blood in here.” said the Lion and the animals dismissed, except for the Monkey that looked at the Brown rat in casual empathy, and did nothing but sigh and sleep.

The next day, due to the unavailability of the White rat, that stayed in its burrow, sleeping, after eating a lot, didn’t go unwasted as there was an entertainment program. The peacocks, with their open wings, danced to the liking of all the animals. The parrots, standing in the middle, imitated the voices of all the animals, which sent them in a thunder of laughter. The hummingbirds hummed the overall development of the case which got interrupted, as they felt it boring at some point. The mouth-opening contest between crocodiles and hippos was a grand success. The staring contest among the sloths subsided as it took too long to judge. The zebras stood one over the other, forming a pyramid, that soon broke down at the fifth level, making them jokers of the wild. The bulls smashed one another's heads for fun. The guerillas made fun of humans by imitating their actions, which was by far the favorite part of the show. The Monkey, who very well knew that the guerillas did wrong actions, went on with the flow without complaining or giving feedback for the gorillas to learn. The day ended with a wild pig, that came with a serious issue, that got pushed on to the next day as it was already too late.

The next day, the Wild pig was all set to speak, and the White rat yawned continuously, whispering to nearby animals, that it was a season for its hibernation, yet it was out because of a serious cause.

"My fellow animals," said the Wild Pig, "I am noticing lately that the human interruption to our forest is on the rise. They took my brother after hitting him with a magic arrow that came out of a small machine in their hand. Humans used to bring huge bows made out of wood and iron, but now the magic arrows are small. It came unseen and took my brother's life. It was fast and deadly. I am afraid every time I wander alone, of a human on my way ready to kill me. I take it that it's not just about me. I am talking to all of you. We have to find a way to this magic arrow."

A shocking revelation, of course, but who's to care. "I think he lost his mind." shouted, the elephant. "How can a small machine threaten a huge animal like me?"

"You can't be so certain without seeing what happened to my brother." the Wild Pig retorted immediately.

"Get out of the way you filthy pig..." the jackal grumbled, saliva dripping in front of its paw "my mouth is all set for a different taste. Don't let me spoil this ground again."

The Pig, considering the fate of Rabbit, subsided, running away into the forest, firmly determined never to return again.

"Is there anybody else, who wishes to bring anything to notice?" asked the jackal. No response.

"Now," said the jackal, assuming itself to be an authority. "Who thinks, Brown rat should be punished?"

All the hands went up in unison. The snake lifted its tongue, the insets- their tentacles, and the birds held their feather on their beaks. Except for the monkey.

The jackal, turning around, angered and disappointed, asked, "Why are not raising your hand?"

"Because I am upside down," said the monkey, slowing closing and opening its eyes.

"Don't you want to raise your hand?" asked the jackal, "don't you want to see Brown rat punished? As you are older than many of us, won't you spill your accumulated wisdom on stage with your judgment,"

"I don't care," sighed the monkey and relaxed, never to show any signs of further reaction.

"Think about it...Your judgment overweighs that any of us as you reside there all the time."

"I don't care," the monkey said, without losing more of its strength.

The Jackal, frustrated at the ape, turned around to the animals and declared, "As you all want to see the Brown rat get punished. It shall be done."

Out of nowhere, popped the tiny mongoose, "What is the punishment? Is it going to finish today?" it asked.

"No! It won't end very easily" shouted the jackal, "the punishment will be decided tomorrow."

That night, the Brown rat, unable to bear the stress, came out of its burrow. The moon was right above its head. The cold wind was not as soothing as it used to be. The monkey was having its supper, carefully sitting over a thick branch, crunching banana, carelessly dropping the peel down below. The Brown rat climbed the tree and unexpected to the monkey, sat in front, lowering its head.

"Am I not worthy to live?" it asked, half of its voice carried away by the wind.

The monkey offered half the banana that was getting inside its mouth, "This is all, I can offer you"

The rat denied and lifted its face, tears marking their depression on tiny hair. "I know that you believe in my innocence."

The monkey, chewing the food said without swallowing the current food, "When did I say that?"

"You supported me by not raising your hand or tail?"

"That's part of my laziness, and why should I support you?" the masticated food fell inside its stomach, and so did the banana peel over a frog under the tree.

"Because I am innocent."

"So?"

"So, you must have helped me. Didn't you see? Everyone was against me, and you knew the truth all along."

The monkey got angry, its eyes enlarged, teeth protruded, and said "First of all, I never knew the truth. So, stop complaining! Second of all, I don't care if someone near is accused. It's chaotic for me to handle any other nonsense."

The Brown rat didn't budge, said raising its voice, "Don't you understand that my life is at stake?"

The monkey leaned backwards, resting its back on the branch, covering its head with both hands, calmly sighed, and began “As I said earlier today...I don’t care,”

“A life is at stake here,”

“Not mine”

The rat, hovered over the Monkey’s stomach, faced it eye to eye, “Don’t you feel anything? Guilt? Don’t you feel guilt?”

“That’s the reason I won’t involve in anything. Listen, as for my experience, I have seen hundreds taking birth and a hundred getting killed one way or the other. Your’s is just one of them.”

The Brown rat felt soo low that it regretted the decision to talk with the Monkey, “What if you are one of them? Your family maybe?”

“I would let it go as an uncontrolled event in this chaotic world. My interaction would only make it more chaotic,”

“Saving life is worthless to you?”

“Not worthless, it’s unnecessary.”

The rat got a raise in depression. Its words amounted to nothing but a stab in its back. “How do you live then?”

“Banana”

“Is that all to your life?”

“Yes...We take birth, we reproduce, we eat, we sleep, we die one day and that’s all.”

“There’s no meaning in being alive?”

“There is...only if you think there is. I prefer not to think there is.”

“What do you think should I do now?” asked the rat, calling it the last question, and felt disappointed before the answer flew out. It waited, but there was no answer.

The next morning, the animals called in for the announcement of punishment, but the Brown rat was nowhere to be found. The jackal, which took the stage announced, “Until we find a rat colored Brown, we will continue to meet here every day to decide on the punishment it deserves."

Every animal, one after the other, came forward to pitch their own idea of punishment.

CHAPTER NINE

THE HAIRCUT

It used to happen every once in three months, especially on Sundays. If that Sunday met with God's birthday or a death of an unfortunate in the village, I had to wait for the next week scratching my head and ears while clearing my forehead from irritating hairs. During these days of unbearable discomfort, my father used to apply a barrel of coconut oil, smash my head like a tabla, and comb them until they were too stiff to adhere to a tornado-like a rock. I had no other way but to wait and suffer.

It was one of these haircuts Sundays that triggered my nerves to burst out of boredom depriving me of much-needed games.

After having a heavy breakfast of half-a-dozen baby rottis and omelets of homebred chicken, I ran to the barbershop with 15Rs in the pockets of my elastic shorts, where my hand retraced every two steps. When I walked confusedly looking at the sky, I had all my friends lined up in the streets, some scratching their chests, picking their noses, biting their nails, and others kicking somebody on the butt. They called me to join the game of The Circle of Caps which I shamefully denied after cursing my hair to fall out never to grow again. The game was too exciting to be missed, where each of us used to collect metal caps of soft drinks, medicine, and liquor bottles, placing them at the edge of the big circle drawn in between the street. We carved and designed rocks that fitted in our palms and one by one, we used to toss them away from the circle. The one with the farthest distance gets to hit the caps first, and all those caps that went out of the circle belonged to the smasher. It was a great business where we formed an alliance and sold our wealth in scrap shops in return for a new steel vessel. Unfortunately, the day I left for a haircut was a dear one as I later heard that the main player Raju was absent. Except for the budding politicians of our street, everyone encouraged us to play and win.

Our tiny village in a remote part of North Karnataka had only one barbershop. It was a great start-up that inspired our villagers to open up their shops in neighboring villages without experience. They learned with failures and scoldings. The one in control of our village was Krishna. Unlike the God who danced on the head of the snake with his flute, this Krishna- the unmarried, danced on his wooden shed with scissors and comb, chewing tobacco and spitting every half a second, suggesting dirty movies to his customers, was no less than a local radio jockey. He knew many things about the villagers. Who hated whom? Who is going to run away with whom? Who was the hot favorite candidate to win the elections? and even those who had a bad stomach were there on his Watch list. His sharp pointy nose was cunning. His eyes always gazed at his customer's pockets and scissors were not immune to cutting the skin of the ears. Anyways, he did his work honestly.

Sundays always attract many people, not realizing this ugly truth I ran there hoping to finish up my haircut and return home as fast as I could to fight with my sister for my favorite show on TV. When I reached the tiny shed at the end of the village where buses arrived, it was already filled with many that I felt hopeless to count. The wooden log behind the wooden chair where unknown customers sat carried hours off of my schedule, which combined with the time Krishna spent spitting his tobacco, would take another half an hour or more for me to reach the precious seat. I sat out on a sand sack folding my hands, and looking blankly at other faces who in turn were looking intensely at the parts of newspapers divided into five pieces. I knew that they couldn't read, but they stared like they were finding grammatical errors. One of them, a huge bearded man with gorilla-like hair, strong arms, and a stout physique looked at me like a police scanning over a suspected thief

"You" he called gruffly "You go to school? What class are you studying?"

"Third standard" I answered politely.

"Can you read this?" he said looking at the paper twitching his forehead.

I jumped at the opportunity and hopped inside the shed, with ample space for me to fit. I stood, stuck in between the bench and wooden chair where the cutting was going on. Drops of hair were raining on me and the dandruff they carried was sufficient to build a sandcastle. I took the newspaper ignoring the hairfall and paused to take a clear look at it. It was an advertisement column. I had a hard time picking the perfect spot to read,

"What should I read?" I asked confusedly.

"Read what you see" the man growled.

Something colorful struck my eyes and I went on to read it not caring about what it was. "Is your partner unsatisfied? Don't worry, use Ramkapuri Pills. One pill for one extra hour on the bed. call 9798739247".

Before I blinked my eyes, the paper was snatched out of my hand, and Krishna was laughing sprinkling red tobacco from each end of his closed mouth. The other men laughed too, squashing paper in their hands, and one young college student with a thick patchy beard patted my back asking me, "Shall I call them for you?". I had no idea what went wrong. I assumed that they had fits, and there was none to stop me from believing that the place was haunted by the ghost of laughter.

The gorilla-like-man who handed me the paper, threw it on the floor and pushed me out of the shed like an angry beast "Krishna?. How much more time?" he screamed with impatience "I had to go to the city?"

Krishna spit the tobacco through the stained window and replied "Why? To meet that doctor?"

The gorilla-like-man rose angrily and went away without looking back, and Krishna maintained his calm demeanor as he very well knew that he would return. Now that relieved me of some time. I felt happy to count the men, there were five in total. If one man consumed 25 minutes + 5 minutes for tobacco going in and out, it would be two and half hours before my turn comes. I waited to count the arriving buses, the passengers from the city dropping off with sweets, farmers with bullock carts, young studs with bikes, responsible faces with cycles, and the hard workers with strong legs. They all amused me for no apparent reason.

There were two, still remaining when the bus came. I had some difficulty wasting time when the scene was empty, but the silence punctuated by the scissor cuts was making a song in my head- the song of newness and letting go of the past. When there was only one man left, the sun was tightly above the head sucking the water out of our bodies. I remembered reading that the sun in that position indicated the time nearing 12PM. I waited anxiously inside the shed, and my bladder called for me to release the storage. I ran behind the shed and realized the true happiness of giving nature back its belonging. I returned back, and the shock awaited me with a man in my seat. I didn't say a word, and I expected Krishna to realize that it was me who must have a haircut before the magic-man. He too was young, fair-skinned with neatly combed hair that covered his ears. To study his face he never lifted his head from the mobile screen.

I had a huge obsession with TV and cursed my father for not letting me watch the TV before going to sleep. I always wished for a tiny TV in hand, to be hidden unnoticed under the blanket. The wish was true! Maybe, God heard me and gave it to this man.

The wooden chair was empty, and as I got up and went in front of the seat, I was pushed away by Krishna "Don't you see the queue?" he was nervous.

"But, I came in the morning" I retorted shyly as I was afraid to voice fearing that I would be sent back without a haircut.

"But, this man is in the queue"

The magic-man rose happily keeping his mobile in his pocket and threw a smile at me.

"Now, sit there and you are next, don't move" Krishna ordered.

I sat stiffly shaking my legs with anger.

The magic-man was continually not responding to Krishna's request to turn and twist his head. It was Krishna who had to bend and twiddle his body to cut the right amount hair. The magic-man behaved as if he was the owner of the shop, which was partly true. I came to know after many years that Krishna was in debt to his father.

The haircut took longer than I anticipated, when the haircut was finished, my excitement was squashed when the shaving cream was spread on his face, I had to wait for some more time.

I picked the newspaper below my foot and tried to understand what I read earlier. That's when I saw the gorilla-like-man ruthlessly approaching me, covering his mouth with his right palm.

He ran into the shop like a burglar "I am next!" he announced and opened his palm, where stood the patches of hair, half cut with bare skin that looked like randomly cut grass in a garden. Krisha laughed, the magic-man smiled, I smiled and the gorilla-like-man was too furious for me to get over joyous. The poor man tried clearing his mustache with a blade but had failed miserably.

"But, the kid is next," Krishna said taking my side for the first time.

The gorilla-like-man tied his lungi and gave a horrendous look into my eyes, which was so strong to get off my mind. His hands itched as he rolled his sleeves and he scratched his beard so roughly that the dust began to fall off of it. I jerked away and let the man sit.

The magic-man emerged as the smartest man I had ever seen. Looking at his hair, I had no doubts he was fit to become a film star. His black hair was combined with erect patches of red hair giving it a funky look. I too decided to have that kind of haircut and imagined myself surrounded by my friends adoring my new look. I just couldn't wait for it to become true, but it was not my turn anymore.

The half-cut gorilla-man turned into the full cut, with no hair left on his face except his eyebrows. He went from gorilla to a monkey.

And finally! It was my turn. Krishna walked out to clear his tobacco. I emerged and sat on the chair that was too low for me to look in the mirror. Krishna arrived, not to catch the scissors in between his fingers but to tell me that he was going to have lunch. He asked me to do the same. I rejected right away, fearing that someone would take my place. Anyhow, I had enough food in the morning to maintain throughout the day.

I was alone, with nothing but the unreachable mirror. I stood up and looked at my face, my body, my clothes, and my eyes. I found that I couldn't look into both of my eyes at once in the mirror, nobody can. My round face with chubby cheeks was elongated longer by an inch by that defective mirror. My neck was squashed under my face. My nose bulged like a dome and my mouth was too small to smile out confidently. My attention went to the color that the handsome man wore, it was sprinkled on the shelf in droplets. I picked it with the tip of my fingers, I erected my hair with the other hand and touched the part of them with the color. My hair was colored red, it looked awesome and after some time, I don't know what changed in me? Somehow I didn't like the look. I rubbed the color: the stain stayed, I sprinkled water and rubbed again: the stain didn't shake. I was in deep trouble, what if Krishna finds out? What if he sends me back? What if he tells my father? I was afraid and the solution that opened up was to cut those stained hairs. I got agitated and my hands shook while I took the scissors which were too big for my finger to hold, and when I placed them on my head, I was even more confused about which direction to move. It took a hell of a lot of patience to coordinate the reflections. I picked a single strand of hair and managed to take it out, and decided to do the same with the rest of them. I improvised to two hairs at a time, then to three, and then to four, and realized there were a thousand more left. When I held a bunch of hairs and moved the scissor to take them out,

“What are you doing?” came a voice from behind.

My body shook at once and a shock wave passed from top to bottom. I turned around abruptly and hid the scissor behind my back. My red hairs were erect and too colorful to be ignored. My heartbeat hammered, and sweat poured down my forehead, two drops from either side, finally marrying below the chin. It was not Krisha, but one of those studs who rode bikes recklessly teasing ladies young and old. He gave a spooky look "What is there in your hands?" he asked.

"Nothing" I stumbled making him curious. I planned to slide the scissor inside the shorts, and when I did, it fell down on the ground passing through it.

“Are you stealing?” the stud asked opening his mobile dialing a number.

“No!” I cried “I was just holding it”

“Who is your father?” he asked, and I knew that with my father’s name I would be in great disaster.

“I was not stealing” I cried again.

"Come down here," he said and I followed down the chair " Do you want me to tell your father? It’s not hard to find him in this village"

I shook my head gently, and the sign of tears was the only expression I wore.

"Then, you have to let me have a haircut, before you" he smiled, trying to convince me.

I nodded and gave up.

Krishna arrived to be surprised at the stud on the seat. "It’s his turn," he said strictly.

"Well, this boy is doing me a favor"

Krishna looked at me for confirmation and I lowered my head.

The cutting went on, me being disturbed, uncomfortable, awkward, and wishing for the color to vanish off my hair. The stud was done and walked out saying nothing but a huge sigh of relief that struck my face like a stone. He really was the lucky man, getting his chance by my mistake. I rose to the seat slowly, worrying that Krisha would look at my hair and scold me off. He did look at the color, raised them up and down, and asked

"What kind of haircut?"

I surely did remember the handsome man "The same, like that handsome man earlier"

"Now, close your eyes and relax. It is going to take a long time" he began sprinkling water over my face and head.

I was happy that something was going in my way and closed my eyes.

The massage began with the cold water, and the cool feeling under that scorching sun unknowingly took me to sleep. I woke up with a slap on my face with the debris of white powder clouding my eyes. I was too excited to look at my hair, I took 15rs out of my pocket and stood up.

When the debris of powder fell, I saw my bald head shining against my eyes and I really did see both of my eyes at once in the mirror.

I also saw my father standing beside me holding those colorful hairs of mine.

CHAPTER TEN

THE MAD.THE MADDER.THE MADDEST.

My head hurts! It felt like my brain was being stabbed by a sharp sword. I could feel my warm blood covering my cheek through my nose and entering my neck. The bright yellow lights from the car posed like a devil's eye teasing my helplessness saying 'the time has come. For the first time in my whole career as a mad pedestrian acting like getting hit by a rich man's car, in turn, blackmailing them for some handsome money has failed. Being homeless is so hard, more than that, living in a big city like Mumbai without these smart risky techniques is like 'Entering into a Lion's cage without a gun'. I tried to stand up, but all the pain in my head had made my broken legs go unnoticed. I sit back with a thud in between the road waiting for death to pull out my soul towards the sky. I couldn't cry, or laugh either, I was confused.

The clock ticked 11 PM and I had never seen suck a big clock in my whole life. Wait! I was on a bed. The bookcase, the flower vase, and a huge screen in front of my eyes made sure that I was not in any hospital. The shiny transparent windows beside the bed reflected all the dominant lights from the city. Was getting hit on a road, a dream? Do I actually belong here? I asked myself and my pulse was up and I welcomed the rise with some hope. The disappointment waited for me below the bedsheet, my legs were bandaged, and so was my head. The smoothness of the surface had blinded my inner pain. The comfort welcomed me but the truth kicked me out. Suddenly, I heard someone's footsteps fading in. I covered my body with the bedsheet at a speed that I never thought possible by any common man. Someone entered the room and stood beside me with their shoes on. I felt him breathing impatiently, his breadth stopped only after hitting my bedsheet. Honestly? I was afraid and didn't make any move waiting for him to walk out. He never did, and I was the loser in the move-to-loose game. I slowly turned straight facing the ceiling and opened my bedsheet.

He was a man of an average height, neatly dressed in his white suit, shaved face, and his hair shined in the dark. His face looked tired, worried and he looked at me in pity, like a doctor would do to his favorite patient. "Are you all right?" he asked with true concern. I simply nodded, he took out his handkerchief and rubbed his unsweaty face. This is how the rich maintain their beauty, I wondered and looked at him without uttering any words from my side. "I am sorry!" he began talking regarding the accident "I was drunk and didn't quite get rid of brakes at the right time". He said it like he really meant it. I nodded again and showed my helplessness again and again making some expressions of bodily pain. "I will take care of you until you are perfect to walk" he confessed and the rush of blood flowed through my cheeks making me a happy man like never before. "Why don't you talk?" he asked "What is your name?" he asked again. I checked my accent from the inside and replied saying my name in my head several times." Sir! I am a homeless" I said and kept cursing myself for not saying my name. I thought he would ask for my name again, but the trick worked as he looked at me like he owed his life. He kept some fruits he was holding all along this time on the table and sat beside me checking the absence of my body parts, and I jerked towards the end of the bed leaving sufficient space for him to sit. I felt comfortable while he sat wearing a smile. He went through his mobile and I stared at the rotating fan and tried guessing the number of wings. My head hurts! Like a sword piercing my brain. "Ahhhhh...!" I screamed trying to bring it under control and the man beside me stood forcing his mobile into his pocket. "Shhhhh !" he signaled to hold his index finger in front of his lips. "Don't scream" he yelled slowly in a painfully suppressed rage as if he was hiding me from someone.

"What's happening there?" A tough male voice came through the walls, I couldn't read the direction. I looked at him in horror, his eyes were reddened, and kept staring at the door as if he was ready to kill the first person to enter. He turned again towards me and this time real sweat had covered his forehead "If you scream again, I will cut you into pieces " he warned me with a bitter tone, I felt alienated and closed my mouth with both of my palms placing one over the another. Did he kidnap me? Or What if he is a drug smuggler, and placed drugs all over the bandages to export me abroad? Thinking about this, I was struck with fear, the cool air from the fan couldn't stop my desperate tears to roll out like waterfalls. Hope for my life was lost, I couldn't run, and my head hurt again "Ahhhhhhhhhh......!" I screamed again, this time with a tight scary noise that can travel for miles. The man beside me without any second thought got hold of my neck and began pressing it with his thumb. I tried to resist with my hand but he was over my body and took full control of it. This time my time had come. I stopped resisting and accepted my death, but the wind flowed peacefully after a moment when he took back his hands turning his head towards the door.

I coughed a few times trying to get hold of air and raised my head to see a huge fat man, aged in his 50s with his red t-shirt and brown shorts. "What is going on here?" he shouted ruthlessly holding a TV remote in his hand. "Dad!! Its....Its...." stuttered the young man standing beside me. "It is my friend .. you see.. he's injured and I helped him...". The old man walked closer to the bed and scanned the bed folding his hands' backside. I kept my normal face without expressing pain and tried to smile.

"Son," the big man said to his son holding his shoulder "Did you take your evening pills?" he asked him calmly. "Yes! father" he answered matching his tone "but, today, I will stay here with my friend" and these words were no less than death to me. If he stays, I was destined to die, if not by suffocation, I will be dead by poisoning for sure.

"Hello, sir?" I said softly to both of them, where only the son turned his face towards me and he looked at his father back and said" My friend needs some help" he said and the old man released his hand from his shoulder and moved a step back from him and 'Slap'. He held his collar and pulled him near the bed and brought his face close to mine. I felt his breadth fast breadth. "Tell me where is your friend?" the old man asked in anger, "Do I look like a mad to you" he declared and pulled him back and slapped again impatiently. The young man was doomed and started crying. I was out of my mind, I couldn't comprehend the faces in the room. One of them tried to kill me while the other never saw me, now both of them are taking on one another.

It's the third vase that he had broken on after the other. The father stood staring like a normal act. The splashes of the soil from the vase all over the floor I escaped some parts of the vase falling on my body too. All these screams and havoc had invited another person towards it. A lady, who might be the old man's wife entered with free hair and held a knife in one hand and an apple in the other. She was not surprised by the disturbance in the room instead he directly marched toward me holding her knife as her protection. "Who are you and how did you get here?" she asked in fear stuck voice maintaining a distance between us "I will call the police now" she picked up the nearest landline and began dialing on it. "Madam please!" I folded my hands "Please listen to my story". My funny helpless face might have convinced her, she kept the landline hanging down and stood facing me." I am sorry !" I begged "Your son standing here had brought me here" her face changed to shock mixed with surprise

"Who?..... My son?" she revolted me with the question and rotated in her place "I live alone you stupid".

Printed by Libri Plureos GmbH in Hamburg,
Germany